(I Just) Died ... Your Arms
Crime Fiction Inspired by One-Hit Wonders
Volume I
Edited by J. Alan Hartman

✶✶✶✶✶✶✶✶✶✶✶✶✶✶✶✶✶✶✶✶✶✶✶✶✶✶✶✶✶✶✶

White City Press

(I Just) Died In Your Arms

Crime Fiction Inspired by One-Hit Wonders
Volume I
Edited by J. Alan Hartman
First published by White City Press
An imprint of Misti Media LLC
https://www.mistimedia.com
Available in both Paperback and eBook Editions
1 2 3 4 5 6 7 8 9 10
Cover design by Safeer Ahmed
Internal Typesetting & Formatting by Willie Chob-Chob Producktions Inkorporated
Copyright © 2024 by each author and Misti Media LLC

Publisher's Note

This is a work of fiction. Names, characters, places, and incidents either are the product of the authors' imagination or are used fictitiously, and any resemblance to actual persons, living or dead, business establishments, events, or locales is entirely coincidental.

The publisher does not have any control over and does not assume any responsibility for author or third-party websites or their content.

Contents

Contents

Play That Funky Music

Introducing
Crime Fiction Inspired by One-Hit Wonders

Sometimes the best ideas come from very simple origins, and the anthology you're about to read is one such case.

I had organized a series of music-themed crime fiction anthologies for another publisher and was thinking about what I might choose as the theme for the next one. Many other editors were doing similar projects, and it was very important that I not do something that some other publisher had already chosen.

A discussion broke out on the Short Mystery Fiction Society blog (https://shortmystery.blogspot.com/) on the topic, as many of the members were either interested in the topic or had been published in a similar anthology. Josh Pachter, who appears in this anthology with his story "The Rapper," offhandedly mentioned that somebody should do an anthology with one-hit wonders.

The term "one-hit wonder" has been used fairly loosely over time, but typically the term refers to a song that hit the top of the music charts and is immediately recognizable by listeners over time, but the artist who created it never had another hit or vanished into the annals of music industry obscurity. Although the term is sometimes viewed as a negative, it really shouldn't be. Some one-hit wonders represent the biggest and most memorable hits to ever grace a radio station or streaming platform. You might not remember Billy Idol's "Cradle of Love" or Barry Manilow's "Weekend in New England," but you know the artist. Chances are you *definitely* know "99 Luftballoons" but have no idea it's by a musician named Nena. "Cradle of Love" and "Weekend in New England" don't get airplay but you can rest assured you'll hear and immediately recognize "99 Luftballoons" when it comes on.

Needless to say, my interest in a one-hit wonder anthology was immediately piqued. Growing up in the 80s, my music collection was positively *packed* with one-hit wonders. That decade was really known for those songs that would stick in your mind but the artist wouldn't. Over the years, I developed a big love affair with the one-hit wonder and would start creating playlists on my various streaming services filled with nothing but these songs. It's a love affair I continue to have to this day.

I resigned as Editor-in-Chief from that other publisher before the anthology could be made, and the new owners decided not to pursue the production of it. But, just like a song that sticks in your head, there was no way I could let this go. When I started up Misti Media this was the first project I resurrected, and I'm so glad that I have. The response from authors was so massive in terms of submissions that I've had no choice but to establish *Crime Fiction Inspired by One-Hit Wonders* as an annual anthology release and new series. Although this first volume is coming out in early 2024, future releases will come out on September 25th each year. This is National One-Hit Wonder Day, and seems the perfect time to release these stories into the wild.

Huge thanks go out to Josh Pachter for the idea nudge, Sandra Murphy for the encouragement to keep it going and John Connor (of Murderous Ink Press) for offering to help get everything put together in the most brilliant way possible.

In addition to these folks, I'm thrilled to be working with old friends Joseph S. Walker, Barb Goffman and Wendy Harrison and I'm truly in love with the writing I discovered through this process from all the other contributors.

So sit back, pop on some earphones (over the ear, please…none of that modern "buds" stuff) and enjoy some classic tunes along with some soon-to-be-classic crime stories.

Jay Hartman
Editor-in-Chief
Misti Media
January 2024

96 Tears
? (Question Mark) &
The Mysterians

Released October 29th 1966
on Pa-Go-Go (7-inch)
Reached #1 on the Billboard Hot 100 in the
US, and the RPM 100 in Canada
Over its long and varied history, the recording has been rated
Billboard #5 for the year 1966, and in 2010 it was listed at #213
on the Rolling Stone *500 Greatest Songs of All Time.*

96 Tears
Vinnie Hansen

If I take the long view, the first tear is for being born. None of this could have happened if my parents hadn't toted home their little bundle of joy. They were going to name me Cynthia. "But we saw your gold hair and blue eyes," my mom said, "and agreed on the spot to Angela."

"Angel Baby," Pops called me.

Tear #2 is for my bad taste in men. What causes that? Aren't we supposed to pick partners who resemble our parents? Pops was a bakery owner with smooth skin and thick hair who smelled like cinnamon rolls. But when I shifted into puberty, my interest in bad boys shot up faster than my body. I hung out behind the junior-high gym, smoking cigarettes and drinking beer with guys, decidedly not the ones who dribbled balls inside.

Tear #3, I shed for that early-acquired taste for alcohol. By high school, I'd graduated to the sophistication and sweetness of alcopops—watermelon and blue—in innocuous bottles like an ice tea drink. The memory summons a primal craving. But there's nothing here in lock-up but Pruno. If I could get the prison wine past my lips, it would do the trick.

Don't cry over spilled milk they say, but lost things are sad: #4 my parents' trust, #5 my excellent grades, and #s 6, 7, 8, 9 and 10 for Shannon, my best friend back in the day. Alienating her deserves wet pillows of regret. She propped me up until it required lying to Mom and Pops, people she'd known since kinder. Senior year, she finally said, "I'm not doing this" and after that, "Your drinking is out of control, Ang."

No one will believe this one, but #11 goes to my looks. Pops gave me flawless skin and thick hair, and my mom a slender build and big eyes. Beauty allowed me to slip through life and cracks.

In high school, I'd been weaving across the rumble strips in my yellow Volkswagen bug—Pops' gift for my Sweet Sixteenth—when a cop pulled me over and swaggered to the window. I rolled my big blues up at him. Five minutes later, I drove away—very carefully—with a warning.

Later, my angel face caused my boss to doubt I could be skimming from the till. The toe of my Chuck Taylors ground against the café floor as he blamed my co-worker Kaleem. So a couple of tears, 12 & 13, for Kaleem. And a few more (14, 15, 16) for others caught in my web of deceit. In the chronicle of my life, they become fuzzier and fuzzier like flies wrapped by the spider and forgotten.

But Brian's clear enough. I skipped over him, (embarrassed, I guess), but yeah, I spilled tears. I was fifteen. Drunk, of course. He was mid-twenties, a known drug dealer, lean and scruffy with a perpetual cigarette hanging from a mean mouth. At a house party, he lounged with one boot planted behind him against a pale yellow wall, smearing dirty shoe prints as he shifted his weight. He observed everyone with shrewd, aloof eyes. Just the kind of guy to make my panties wet.

"Wanna go upstairs?" That was his pick-up line.

In a large bedroom with a perfectly straight, striped comforter over a king-sized bed and thick, fluffy towels in the adjoining bathroom, he casually ended my virginity. That's one tear (17). I wished later that more pomp and circumstance had accompanied the event, but I didn't cry about it. The bawling, 18, 19, 20, 21, came when I woke up. I left the bathroom not quite so pristine and crept down the stairs. Brian had resumed his post. The sleaziest girl at my high school had her arms twined around his neck.

He viewed me over dark roots of peroxided hair. Then he returned to lashing her studded ear with his tongue.

There were plenty of guys after Brian but they're a blur. No

4

waterworks for them.

Tears 22 to 26 are for Mrs. Carmichael, my senior-year English teacher, a strict, skinny old woman who started class at the bell and spent the hour whipping us into scholars, who made us write, in class, with eagle eyes for anyone trying to access CliffsNotes on a phone. She called on everyone, hand up or not, after allowing fair warning to gather their thoughts. You best be mustering some.

Mrs. Carmichael valiantly tried to save me, to resurrect the alert, curious student I'd been as a child. You've probably all had one teacher like that who sees your "potential."

She detained me regularly. I'll never forget her line, "This essay is wholly inadequate," *tapping the single sheet of paper with her pen* "but this line" *kissing her fingertips* "is sublime."

Bittersweet, the word, was invented for that moment. As I write with my stubby prison pencil, I wonder what she'd think of this piece. If she could look down from heaven, would she be disappointed to see me here? Even though I never did one thing to thank her or to make her remember me, Mrs. Carmichael never forgot her "charges," as she called us.

I mourn, let's say 27-32, for the screwed-up thinking I might find Mr. Right in a Wrong Place. In my core, I yearned for a relationship like my mom and Pops's. Sure, they bickered—my mom frustrated by the demanding hours of running a bakery, and Pops not fully appreciating, I suppose, that she was the primary one raising me and my two younger brothers, running the house on top of helping with the business—waiting on customers and doing the books—much less fun, I imagine, than inventing recipes and baking in the kitchen. Still, they never went for an evening walk without holding hands, and Pops called her "Buttercup."

Since I wasn't going to college, I wanted, at least, to be someone's buttercup. Before I graduated, I met Rendell in the park by our high school in a hidden spot where teenagers went to conduct certain transactions. That twist of fate deserves a deluge of tears, 33, 34, 35, 36,

37, 38, 39, 40, 41, 42, 43, 44, 45, 46, my whole supply if there weren't other things to wash clean. I wouldn't have been in the Wrong Place if Shannon hadn't said, "I'm not doing this," because she'd seen me sneak sips from a flask during Government class. After school, she'd driven off without me, leaving me with no ride home, so I meandered down to the circle of packed dirt hidden in the trees. And there Rendell sat on a fallen branch.

He was gorgeous: slouchy with full lips and broad shoulders. But more importantly, he had panache. Panache is like Tabasco. Sprinkle on enough and I'll scarf up a four-day-old meatloaf.

Rendell would have called me "Buttercup" or anything else my heart desired. As long as I didn't disrupt his lifestyle of using his looks and charm to sponge off women as he indulged in drugs and sports betting. He knew how to stroke my ego and my body. That took us quite a way. Years, actually, through my post high-school jobs that led to working at a bar and learning to bartend.

But I suppose, deep down, I wanted more than a grungy apartment. As drawn as I was to bad boys, I liked a good mattress. When Rendell was arrested for a burglary and wanted me to dump my savings into his jail commissary account, I vamoosed.

San Francisco. Like my men, more a romantic than a wise choice. Tear 47 for fog and freezing wind whipping down narrow streets. I'd come from the Salinas Valley with no idea I'd never feel warm again. Tear 48 for the cost! I rented a room in a house shared with four housemates. One bathroom.

Tear 49 for my second job in an Irish bakery on the edge of Noe Valley, doing the same drudgery as my mom, but without meaning, neither supporting a partner's passion nor providing for a family. And tear 50 because my parents told me Shannon had graduated with an MA in English, had returned to our town to teach, and had married a hometown boy, one of those who dribbled balls inside the junior high gym and had come back to coach at the high school. Would I ever have a family? Did I want to have a family?

In a way bad grades and bad men never could, my parents' happiness for Shannon—the contrast of her lightness with my darkness—shamed me all the way to AA. Shannon, unknowingly, to my rescue—again.

It would be more in sync with my life story if I had met Guillermo (tears 51 and many more) where I bartended, but instead he came into the bakery for soda bread. Every Sunday after the late service at St. Paul's. No matter how long the line of old Irish women and chatting Latinas from the Mission, he'd wait.

Then I'd ring up his loaf of soda bread.

He'd pay, his large brown eyes heavy-lidded. Were those what they called bedroom eyes? He was older. Thirty? Forty? Dark, curly hair. No ring. But a loaf of bread was too much for a single man, and an aura of guilty married man radiated from him like a force shield. I silently made change.

"You could be nicer to the customers," Mrs. Kelly said.

"You should ring him up."

Mrs. Kelly squinted at me. "Did Mr. Vicario do something?"

How could I explain to the plump, rosy-cheeked, middle-aged woman that Guillermo Vicario's eyes feasted on more than Irish oat cookies?

But I didn't buy the gun because of Guillermo Vicario. I bought it because of Rendell.

He stumbled into the bar where I worked. Literally stumbled, not happened upon. It wasn't that kind of place. The Down Under was an unyuppified dive, dark and narrow, with a clientele of regulars stooped inside wraiths of prohibited smoke. Seasoned drinkers, they sometimes passed out but seldom puked. I liked bartending there because it was uncomplicated.

Until Rendell showed up.

"Buttercup." Those gorgeous full lips pulled into a sloppy smile. During our years together, I'd made the mistake of sharing certain details. The first time he'd tried out *Buttercup* on me, I'd thought he was too dense to understand I wanted the affection behind the nickname; I didn't want to be called by my mom's nickname. On the second go, I understood he knew exactly what he was doing. He was ridiculing my longing. Ridiculing the tenderness Pops showed my mom.

There was only one reason for Rendell to be in the Down Under, and it wasn't to drink the domestic beer he ordered.

So although I could have spent all my remaining tears on Guillermo, I've reserved a few (let's say 80-85) for the shit show of life that plopped Rendell down in front of me and had him catch himself on the bar as he half slid off the stool.

Then up to tear 90 for the Smith and Wesson revolver. Tears in hindsight, of course. When I took BART to an East Bay gun shop the next day, it seemed like the right thing to do. The train whooshed into the dark tunnel under the bay, the invisible crushing weight of water above like Rendell—out there, hanging over my life, threatening. Rendell was an unscrupulous human being, a convicted felon, stalking me where I worked. Protection seemed like a good idea.

I loaded bullets in a chamber, preferring that meditative task to slapping in a magazine. The salesman eagerly gave me a tutorial and sent me home with a pamphlet on gun safety to begin my ten-day waiting period.

That night, Rendell returned to the Down Under as I knew he would. "You tore my heart out."

I plunked down his beer and turned away.

"Angel Baby," he tried this time.

I whirled, unable to control myself. "Don't call me that."

"Or what?" he smirked. "You'll have the bouncer toss me?"

There was no bouncer, of course, only my regulars in various stages of inebriation, and Berto, who washed glasses, didn't speak English, and acted like ICE might appear any second. How long ago did Rendell leave our hometown? Did he know how sick my father was? Was he striking for my jugular or was it just more of his teasing? Was I overreacting, playing right into his hands?

"It was shitty to leave me high and dry like that, Ang."

"Dry?" I snorted. "Right." I should have kept walking along the bar. I should not have responded.

"Why are you so cold? I think about you every night."

If that were true—highly unlikely—but if it were, the reason for it would not be pleasant. I swung around to pick up a bar towel.

"How much does that second job make ya?"

I froze. How did he know about that? Halfway down the bar, a regular tapped the wood to indicate he wanted another shot. I picked up the Jack Daniels and moved along the counter, my legs stiff. I came back near Rendell to return the bottle. As much as I wanted to know how he'd found out about my job at the bakery, engaging with him would be stepping into quicksand. Instead I said to Berto, "¿Hay rodajas de limón?"

Berto looked at me bug-eyed. He'd already sliced up one lemon and we were unlikely to use that, except in my own glasses of sparkling water. But anything not to talk to Rendell. I wiped down the counter, dark wood with heavy lacquer over chips and scratches.

"Remember Mrs. Carmichael?"

My arm stopped mid-rotation. I never understood how Rendell could be such a loser when he always seemed to have an ace up his sleeve.

I continued cleaning and waited.

"She's dead."

The blow missed its mark. Mrs. Carmichael had been working past the age when most teachers retired; over the years the idea she could be dead had crossed my mind.

Ginger, a middle-aged redhead at the end of the bar, raised her glass to indicate another vodka tonic. As she leaned into the beefy shoulder of a man, her low-cut sweater snugged her body—sexy without screaming streetwalker.

Before I swung around to fix Ginger's drink, Rendell said, "Run over by our local drug dealer." He worked his tongue around his teeth, relishing the story. "Guy named Brian."

This punch landed home.

Rendell chuckled. Watching me, he took a swig of beer and licked his lips. His presence made me itchy for a drink. At AA meetings, attendees advised me to quit bartending, to which I pointed out San Francisco was second only to Buffalo for per capita bars, part of the reason I'd moved to The City. "If I decide to drink, being one block rather than one foot from the booze isn't going to stop me."

I shoveled ice cubes into a glass, stirred in vodka and tonic, added a twist of lime and delivered the drink, lingering with Ginger and her "date," asking how they were doing tonight.

"Fine, darling." Ginger lowered thickly painted lashes, sucked her drink, and subtly shook red curls at me. Not tonight. She was working.

Mr. Jack Daniels had let his forehead collapse to arms crossed on the bar—not passed out, just weighed down, as though the burdens that sagged his skin and rounded his shoulders had won this round.

When I tried to walk past Rendell, he lifted off the stool and lurched to grab my arm. I executed a nifty pirouette. "Keep your hands off me."

Jack Daniels whipped his head up and Ginger's man half rose from his stool. We may not have had a bouncer but I was surrounded by protective drunks.

"It's okay," Rendell said to them, making *down-boy* motions and smiling. "We've known each other a loooong time. Haven't we, Angel Baby?"

Good thing there was a ten-day waiting period on that gun.

Well nine days now.

*****

The next day, Rendell dragged himself into the bakery with the chime of the bell and a gust of San Francisco chill. He looked around with amusement and sniffed the air. "Reminds me of your pop's place."

I ignored him. Mrs. Kelly frowned at me, her steely blue eyes telling me to get my butt up to the counter to help this customer, never mind his rumpled shirt and disheveled hair.

Since I wasn't budging, Mrs. Kelly stepped forward. "May I help you?"

"A shortbread cookie, please. They look amazing."

From behind Mrs. Kelly's broad back, I glared at Rendell.

He took the cookie and sat at one of the little round tables. For the moment there were only the three of us inside the store. He quirked his brows at me. "You knew him, right?"

That's the weird thing about having been involved with a person. Our last conversation had ended twelve hours ago but I knew exactly what Rendell was talking about and who he meant. The local drug dealer. The one who killed Mrs. Carmichael. *Brian.*

His salivating was more about torturing me than the shortbread cookie.

I didn't answer. I was thinking how the smallness of that town had allowed pieces of my life to collide like a demolition derby. Now Rendell was taunting me with the wreckage. Like he was somehow the final car. The winner.

*****

Rendell continued to stalk me. I counted the days until I'd be the owner of the "pre-owned" revolver. I fantasized about what might happen. Nothing if Rendell left his performance at tormenting. But that wasn't how Rendell operated. In his head, I owed him something and he'd come to collect.

On my day off from the bakery, I drove my now rusted and dented Volkswagen Bug to pick up the Smith and Wesson and a box of ammo. I put the gun in the cargo hold to carry home, but in my rented room, I cleaned out my favorite tote to make space for the weapon, the lack of a concealed-carry permit the least of my worries.

If Rendell followed me when the bar closed, I would lead him into an alley and pull the weapon. Maybe fire a shot near his foot and say, "You never could dance." A wonderfully satisfying thought.

Rendell showed up that night, but it was Saturday, the place packed with customers, and Jordan, a professional bodybuilder, was tending bar with me. I'd tipped him off about Rendell. Jordan glided down the bar and gave Rendell an unfriendly, "Whatdayawant, dude?"

Rendell left.

He reappeared at the bakery as the church crowd thinned, stepping through the door behind Guillermo.

As usual, Guillermo doffed his hat and stood staring at me with moony eyes.

"Are you going to order sometime today?" Rendell said.

Guillermo asked for his usual loaf of soda bread. I handed him the paper bag. He waited.

Rendell muttered, "She's not interested, buddy."

Guillermo surprised me, "And a cup of coffee, please."

I fetched it slowly, in no hurry to wait on Rendell.

Guillermo fumbled through his coins as he often did. Behind him Rendell shifted his weight and ran through his limited repertoire of expressions—lips folding inward, shoulders tensing, eyes narrowing.

I took Guillermo's bills and poured some change from the tip jar. "I've got it," I said.

"Oh," Guillermo murmured, shaking his head, "no, no, no."

Rendell pressed close behind him. "She's got you covered, Jack."

Guillermo swung around, Rendell in so tight that Guillermo slammed into him like a football tackle.

Rendell staggered and drew back a fist. Mrs. Kelly—emerging from the back room and carrying a tray of apple cakes—said: "What might be going on here?"

When I reached under the counter and came up with my Smith and Wesson, all the cakes poured onto the floor.

I pointed the gun at Rendell. "You need to leave."

Rendell side-stepped Guillermo as though he were irrelevant. "Or what?" He smirked. His attention riveted on me now. "Angel Baby." He sneered at my Pop's loving pet name for me, took all that was sweet and holy in my life, and smeared it like shit.

That's when I fired.

And that's when Guillermo shoved Rendell aside.

And that's why I cry ... cry, cry, cry for Guillermo, dead on the bakery floor.

Guilty of second-degree murder, I count down my time and my tears.

The 96th is for me.

Na Na Hey Hey Kiss Him Goodbye
Steam

Na Na Hey Hey Kiss Him Goodbye reached #1 in the United States for two weeks, on December 6 and 13, 1969. It was *Billboard*'s final multi-week number 1 hit of the 1960s and also peaked at #20 on the soul chart.

In Canada, the song reached number six.

By the beginning of the 21st century, sales had exceeded 6.5 million records, attaining mulit-platinum record status.

Kiss Him Goodbye
Jeanne DuBois

Tonya Clarke Cassidy (tall, dark, corkscrew curls) hears a vehicle out front and leaves off assembling the salad to take a peek. A blue sedan is parked at the curb. A Black man in a suit stands on the sidewalk, eyeing the neighborhood. It's a quiet one, inhabited by young families as well as retirees, part of a planned unit development designed in the early Sixties. Her bungalow could use another coat of turquoise paint, but the metal roof is new, the grass mowed, and flowers bloom red in the shifting shade of the pines.

"Is there a problem?" Jack asks, watching her at the window.

"A man in a suit is walking up the path. Is that a problem in your world, Jack?"

"Crap," Jack says and heads for his hidey-hole. Her ex-husband's a good-looking guy. Too bad he's such a PITA. When he said he needed a break from his high-pressure job (he sells building materials) and asked to bunk in with their son for a couple weeks, Tonya said fine. But whenever someone knocks at her door, he disappears. Tonya suspects a jealous husband is to blame, despite his denials. She glances at ten-year-old Willie now, reading at the kitchen table, and is happy to see his eyes still focused on his book. Willie's skin is dark like hers, but his hair is blond and curly, like his dad's.

"Could be another realtor, the market is looking up," Tonya says to nobody but herself. Jack's in the pantry, Mia's in her bedroom, Willie's deaf, and Butterscotch, Willie's therapy dog, is at the groomer's.

Tonya opens the front door to the knock, a question on her heart-shaped face.

"Tonya Cassidy?" he asks. His eyes are bright, his lashes long and silky. "From Dunnellon?"

Dunedin. But whatever. "Who's asking?"

He flashes a badge. "Sheriff's Deputy Duwayne Washington. I had a hard time finding you."

Tonya crosses her arms. These boys and their games. "Why'd you need to find me?"

He gets right to business. "When did you last see your husband?"

"Ex-husband. Can't remember."

"We can do this down at the station."

"What station is that, Duwayne, the one for the tourist trolley?"

He frowns at her, half-angry, half-confused.

"Your badge says St. Joe's Florida, not St. John's County. And that suit and tie?" Tonya shakes her head. "Where'd you think you were playing, *Midsomer Murders*?" Not that it ever featured dark-skinned people, unlike *Vera*, where actors seemed to be cast based on character rather than skin color. Tonya moves to close the door.

"Okay, okay, wait, here's the real deal." He presses his palms together and lowers his voice. "Your husband owes some bad people money, and they're not going to stop till he pays it back. Now, I'd be willing to be your intermediary, for a small fee."

"Uh, huh. How much we talking here? Fifty? A hundred-fifty?"

Duwayne looks away. "He owes forty-five thousand. I'd need five on top of that."

Tonya laughs. "Keep dreaming. I don't have that kind of money."

"What about your son's insurance settlement?"

Tonya's heart freezes. It must show on her face, because he strings his next words together: "Yournextvisitorcouldbearealbad—"

Tonya closes the door, turns the deadbolt, and watches him through one of the sidelights. He ambles back to the sedan, slides in behind the wheel, takes one last look at her, and drives away. Returning to the kitchen, Tonya discovers Jack sitting across from Willie at the table, trying to do American Sign Language. A huge difference from before their divorce two years ago when Jack was still fighting to get Willie double cochlear implants (eight months after the car accident, with Jack driving, that cost their son his hearing) as opposed to hearing aids and ASL tutoring.

Willie uses his voice now, a rare occurrence. It's loud. Willie doesn't know, he can't hear it. "Daddy, do your hands like this." He slowly signs, TIME FOR DINNER, I'M HUNGRY.

Jack signs it back to him. Willie grins and waves both hands (Deaf claps) to say good job. Her heart thaws.

Later, when the kids are in their rooms asleep, or making clandestine TikTok videos in Mia's case, Tonya asks Jack point-blank if he's there to get a share of Willie's insurance money to pay off a debt. Jack blinks blue eyes and says he doesn't owe anybody money, well, not enough to worry about, probably, but he'd like to open a motorcycle repair shop, and couldn't he use some of the insurance money for that?

"Since you wouldn't let Willie get the implants," Jack said, "that money's just sitting there."

Tonya works on keeping her temper in check. She doesn't want Mia to hear her yelling and get upset. "The money's not just sitting there. We use it for doctor visits, hearing aids—"

"That don't cost a hundred fifty-eight thousand dollars."

"The money is for Willie," Tonya says, noting that Jack has correctly quoted the total of Willie's three accounts. A twitch starts in her right eye. "He might decide he wants implants when he's older."

Jack scoffs, "I thought you wanted nothing to do with CIs."

"I wanted him to learn sign language so he could go to a Deaf school and make friends. Cochlear implants do not restore normal hearing, they destroy residual hearing, and they're not reversible." She's told Jack this so many times it comes out of her mouth like a recording. "Willie's brain would need a couple years to learn how to process its electronic sounds. How was he supposed to communicate in the meantime?"

Jack says, "You used some to buy this house."

Back to the money. Safer ground. "I did," Tonya says, after a minute of Herculean self-restraint and objective reflection. "Twenty-five thousand. Is that enough to start a motorcycle repair shop?"

"Hell, yeah. I got a guy interested in going in with me. Duwayne'll put up the other twenty-five." Jack is positively beaming.

"Duwayne Washington?"

Jack stares at Tonya in disbelief. "You know him?"

She shares the details of her encounter with the fake deputy.

"He made that badge online," Jack says, smiling. "It was Halloween and he was going as one of those YMCA guys."

Tonya raises her eyebrows.

Jack asks, "What?"

"You told him about Willie's insurance money." It's not a question.

"I mighta done, yeah. But I sure as hell never said he should come here and try to squeeze some of it out of you. He's supposed to come up with his own twenty-five thousand. I don't know what he was thinking."

"He was thinking he gets the whole fifty from me, you two are home free."

"I'll talk to him," Jack promises. "He's not a bad guy. He's young. He doesn't always think things through."

Sounds familiar. "Jack, I think it's time you either went home or moved into an Airbnb. I know you want to see the kids, but I'm not comfortable with you staying here anymore."

Abashed, Jack sinks into the cushion. "I'll go online and see if I can find a place."

"Use your phone," Tonya says.

"Yes, ma'am."

Tonya heads to her room to change all her computer passwords.

*****

Tuesday is mayhem. Willie's bus is late picking him up for school. A parent is lying in wait for Tonya behind a tree in the school parking lot. An unannounced fire drill occurs during a test in the third period. Half of the fourth period comes straight from PE without deodorant. Her interactive white board goes dark in the fifth period and Gary Jones, the IT guy, who seems to be in her back pocket every other day, is nowhere to be found. The principal does a surprise walk-through during the sixth period and wants to talk about it after school. Argh.

Tonya races home to collect Willie and Butterscotch and drive them to the park in time for Mia's softball game, only to discover Jack won't be able to move out until Thursday, and the dog has rolled in something dead.

Tonya wails, "I hate this day!"

"Butterscotch didn't kill the squirrel," Jack says, misunderstanding. "It was flat as a pancake."

"I can't take her to the groomer's now, Mia has a game." Tonya's so frantic she actually considers asking Jack to carry the eighty-pound golden-doodle to the groomer on his motorcycle.

Luckily, Jack suggests an alternative. "I can give Butterscotch a bath while you're gone."

"You'll have to bathe her in the tub. She'll get muddy if you use the hose."

"Okay."

"You'll have to dry her with a blow dryer until she's completely dry or else she'll get a rash."

"I can do that."

Tonya touches Willie's shoulder to get his attention. BUTTERSCOTCH STINKS. YOU STAY HOME WITH HER AND DADDY?

NO, Willie signs emphatically, TODAY CHESS! Ray Martinez, a (handsome) Deaf man, comes to the park on Tuesdays to play chess with him (and to flirt with her, nothing serious, not even coffee, though she plans to invite him over for a meal, to thank him, when Jack's vacation is over).

Tonya signs, HAVE YOUR PHONE?

YES, Willie signs, patting his shorts pocket.

21

"Willie's coming with me," Tonya tells Jack, signing for Willie, who hugs his father, then races for the car.

"See you soon, buddy," Jack calls after him, "I love you!"

Tonya says, "You know he can't hear you, right?"

Jack looks at her, stricken.

Tonya relents. "Don't worry, I'll tell him what you said."

"Hey," Jack says, as she's turning away, "Duwayne says that wasn't him yesterday. He was at work till seven."

"Whatever."

*****

Surrounded by several hundred wooded acres, the county park includes two ball fields (Mia's team is warming up on one), a soccer field, several hard courts, a fitness/nature trail, a skatepark, a playground, and a covered picnic area. Tonya parks in the paved lot, which isn't full (only because it's a weekday afternoon), and leads the way to the softball field. Willie takes his leave from there, after finding fourteen-year-old Mia and giving her a lucky hug, their pre-game routine.

Tonya touches Willie's shoulder, and when he looks at her, she signs, PHONE ON?

Willie holds it up to show her.

O-K. Tonya watches him walk to the picnic tables. His blue hearing aids are as bright as beacons in the afternoon sun. Willie waves when he arrives, then turns his back to take his seat on the concrete bench. Ray, recognizable in his signature white long-sleeve shirt and brown cotton vest, acknowledges Tonya with a wave of his own, and she relaxes.

Mia starts the game at first base. Her best friend April is starting on third and overthrows Mia on the first play. On the next play, Mia takes her foot off the base, reaching to catch a ball thrown wide by the shortstop. Things go downhill from there. The opposing team scores five runs before Mia's team can get three outs. In the bottom of the first, Mia whiffs her first three pitches and stomps back to the dugout, tugging on her braids. Her daughter's head is going to hurt tonight,

Tonya reflects wryly.

Kelly, red hair and wrinkles, a teacher Tonya knows from school district math workshops, plops on the bleacher next to her. "Happy Tuesday."

Tonya smiles at her. "Aren't you sitting on the wrong side?"

"Too sunny over there, thank you very much. Your organist isn't coming?"

"I guess not," Tonya says, craning her neck to see the next-to-top row of the bleachers where Gary Jones usually sits in his Indiana Jones hat, iPad on his lap, portable speaker perched nearby. "He wasn't in school today."

"Oh, darn, I was looking forward to those cute little walk-up songs he plays for all the girls. Though I won't miss hearing 'Na Na Hey Hey' whenever we make a pitching change." She laughs. "It's nice how he comes out and supports your team."

Tonya wants to say, I think he's stalking me, his van is always in my neighborhood, but settles for, "I think he lives nearby."

Two fly balls and the teams switch sides. The first batter gets a piece of every pitch. The count is still 0-2 after five minutes.

"My daughter's up next," Kelly says, pointing to the on-deck circle. "Ooo, I thought that one was going to be fair. Where's Willie?"

"Playing chess."

"I don't see him."

"Over there." Tonya glances at the picnic table as she gestures, then stands for a better view. She can make out chess pieces and a board, but there's no sign of Ray or Willie. That's never happened before. A shiver runs up her spine. "If I'm not back, tell Mia to go with April."

Kelly waves a hand. "You worry too much."

Except that it's not like Tonya can call Willie's name and he'll come running. She texts him on her way. No reply.

Standing at the deserted table, Tonya surveys the area in all directions. To the south, a sidewalk leads to the hard courts. West, it's back to the ballfields. To the north, the playground and parking lot.

East, a boardwalk goes over the creek to the fitness/nature trail. A young woman jogs off the boardwalk now, straight into Tonya's outstretched arms. White cords trail from her ears. She is more surprised than annoyed by the human blockade.

Tonya asks, "Did you see a man and a boy on the boardwalk?"

"No, I was the only one."

Tonya checks her phone again for messages. Finding none, she texts Willie a second time, pockets her phone, and heads for the hard courts, the site of the nearest drinking fountain.

"Nobody came this way," the tennis players say.

Tonya pivots and goes to the playground. A white woman is there, pushing a toddler on a baby swing.

"A man and a boy passed by a little bit ago," she says.

Two Black teens are working on a bicycle in the shade on the fitness trail. Tonya runs across the parking lot to talk to them. They gesture toward the playground.

"They're not at the playground," Tonya says.

"Restroom," the taller one says.

And sure enough, hidden in the shade of an old oak, Tonya finds a squat concrete building with a chained-open door. Above the opening, a sign: *Women*. Next to the opening, is a braille plaque. Inside, two stalls, two sinks, and one changing table. No Willie.

Tonya trips around the outside of the building. The grass is longer here. Weeds clog the base of the hill behind it. She finds another door in the back with a sign: *Men*. But the door is closed and there is no handle to open it, only a lock plate, without a key, and two pieces of chain secured to an anchor in the ground with a padlock. Tonya pounds the door with her fists until she hears a faint banging inside the room.

"My son is locked in the men's room," she shouts at the first person she sees, a spindly white man in pink shorts, jogging down the hill. He does a quick one-eighty and is out of voice range before she can say another word. Tonya smooths down her hair as she emerges from the shade. Mustn't scare the villagers.

She's staring at her phone, trying to decide if she should press 9-1-1 or the Emergency button when a County Parks truck stops on the grass in front of her.

A big Black man in work clothes slides out, jangling a ring heavy with keys. "What seems to be the trouble here?"

The jogger reappears as if by magic, brandishing his phone, and greeting the Parks man before Tonya can speak. "There you are. I've been calling the main office. I kept getting an answering machine."

"They got all your messages," the big man says dryly. "They radioed me right away. They don't close down till five, but sometimes the phone gets busy at the end of the day. I'm not sure what—"

"Stop and listen." Tonya uses her most authoritative teacher voice, the one she saves for things like Armed Intruder alerts and End of Course exams. If she sounded like this all the time, the kids would tune her out the way she does Gary Jones whose blah-blah-blah is like an everyday Greek chorus. "My son is locked inside the men's room. You have to unlock the door. Now."

"All right, already." The amount of energy the big man is conserving with his tortoise-like movements could run a third-world country for a week.

The jogger pushes past her, pounds on the men's room door, hollers through the steel, "Don't worry, we're coming," then turns toward Tonya with a sparkling (he thinks) smile.

A scary thought flits through Tonya's mind, not the one where she's choking the jogger with her bare hands. No, it's about the chain, what her dad would call a logging chain, once used to keep the door open. It's been cut. Tonya pokes in the weeds with her shoe while the men guess-and-check their way through the keyring.

Tonya asks impatiently, "Why isn't there a way to open the door from the inside?"

"Rusted," says the big man.

As the men's room door inches open, Tonya's knees weaken with relief. But Willie isn't inside. Only Ray. Oblivious to the mind-altering confusion caused by his appearance ("That's your *son*?"), Ray pulls Tonya away from the building.

When they're out of sight, Ray shoves a folded note into her hands and signs, BLACK MAN SNATCH (he means kidnapped, Tonya thinks wildly) WILLIE.

With trembling fingers, Tonya unfolds the note.

call the cops and he's a dead boy

The playground dissolves into an impressionist painting. Next thing Tonya knows, she's on a bench, head between her knees, trying to remember how to breathe. When she can sit up, she phones Jack. It goes straight to voicemail. His mailbox is full. She sends him a text: *Call me!*

Ray waves a hand in her face. When she looks at him, he signs, LET'S GO.

Tonya lurches to her feet. They cross the parking lot. She scans the occupied spaces. There are no blue sedans. But there's a blue truck, a big one, with an extended cab full of stuff. In the truck bed, camped out on a lawn chair, sits a Black woman with a cap of tight gray curls, dressed in olive drab. She's been up there overseeing the parking lot every Tuesday and Thursday afternoon for three weeks, or as long as softball has been going on, and hasn't returned a single greeting Tonya's tossed her way.

Tonya decides to give it another try. She yells as she nears the truck, "Did you see a man with a boy wearing blue hearing aids?"

The woman does not deign to glance in Tonya's direction. An osprey screeches from the sky somewhere behind them. A moment later, the woman lifts a large pair of binoculars to her eyes. If only I were a bird, Tonya thinks.

Ray bangs on the side of the truck until the woman looks down at him, then signs, BLACK MAN SNATCH DEAF BOY. YOU SEE THEM?

NO, the woman signs, SORRY.

Tonya feels heat flooding her face. No wonder the woman didn't respond. Tonya signs her query: YOU SEE A BLUE CAR?

The woman regards Tonya for a moment before signing, NO BLUE CAR. YOUR SON?

Tears leak from Tonya's eyes. MY SON.

Ray signs, THANK YOU, and urges Tonya back toward the restroom building.

A minute later, the woman in olive is alongside, fingerspelling her name, P-A-T-T-Y W-O-L-F-E, binoculars at the ready.

*****

The uphill path behind the men's room splits when it reaches the top, heading either left to the skatepark entrance or down through the trees to the fitness/nature trail. Ray goes down the hill and they follow. There are lots of birds in the woods and squirrels. Probably snakes and spiders, too. Sounds tickle Tonya's eardrum from time to time, but Ray is already many yards ahead. They catch him when he stops to point out a shoe print in the sand at the edge of the trail, much smaller than his shoe, with a patterned sole.

WILLIE? Tonya asks Ray.

Ray replies, MAYBE.

The fitness trail loops right, but Ray cuts through the trees. A flash of blue stops her heart for a second. But it's only a jay. And then they're stepping out of the woods onto a dirt road striped with sunlight. Patty plants herself in the center of the road and focuses her binoculars in both directions.

She signs excitedly, BLUE CAR, and points.

Ray waves them back into the woods. They follow in his footsteps, keeping out of sight. Soon they are there, staring at patches of blue through a screen of trees. Patty checks out the car with her binoculars, then hands them to Ray with a worried glance at Tonya. Tonya surges toward the road, ignoring the cuts on her legs from thorns, falling finally, tripped up by vines. It takes a few seconds to untangle herself. Her two companions are already by the car when she bursts from the trees. Ray warns her not to touch anything.

Tonya circles the blue sedan. Its trunk lid is up. One backdoor is open. No one is in the trunk. No one is in the back seat. Tonya peers in the driver's tinted window. Duwayne Washington is slumped sideways behind the wheel. There are bolt cutters on the passenger seat, long ones, heavy-duty. And blood. Lots of it. Tonya backs away, squeezing her eyes shut.

When she opens them, Ray and Patty are gone.

Stop and think, she tells herself and looks around. The only tire tracks in the area belong to the blue sedan. All the footprints, except for those that come from the park and stop at the car, head back into the woods. Tonya follows them in, hoping for a sign. She finds one. Her phone. She frees it from its nest of vines, brushes it off, and checks her messages. There's one from Willie.

See my real-time location on Maps

Something warm brushes Tonya's arm. She screams and jumps. It's only Ray. Patty's behind him. He's removed his shirt but retained his vest. Tattoos darken both his arms. He gives her the blue hearing aid Patty found in the woods. Tonya's spirits soar. She tucks it safely away in her bra, shows them the text, and clicks on the link. Willie's photo appears in a teardrop, marking his location on a map. She presses the button for *Directions*. A dotted line pops up on the map, showing her the way. The miracle of GPS. Thank you, Dr. Gladys West.

Willie's teardrop places him inside a small gray square with a short tail located in the southeast corner of the much larger green park area. A seven-minute walk away. While Tonya negotiates two sides of the right triangle, Ray will traverse its hypotenuse, through the woods, with Patty. Her binoculars have a compass.

Tonya can't remember how to sign, her brain's too busy blocking out a million scary thoughts, so she says, "Good luck to us," in English, and gives them a thumbs-up.

Patty waves goodbye with a hopeful smile, Ray squeezes Tonya's arm, and they're gone.

Tonya follows the dotted line out of the woods, jogging past the blue sedan and on and on until she comes to a narrow lime rock road full of potholes (the little tail) where she swerves left. Both sides of this road are blooming with wildflowers, yellow mostly, with some pink, an auspicious beginning to her final path of doom. Straight ahead, according to the map, is where she'll find Willie. But she's an adult. She's faced the reality. The only thing she's sure to find is his phone.

*****

Tonya steps over the yellow caution tape. There's a weathered sign, *LONE OAK CAMP*, beside the entrance. It lies. Oak saplings crowd the edges of the pockmarked concrete. A blue tarp shines from a slanted roof across the square. Trees block the rest of her view of the building. The square is strewn with leaves and twigs. Tonya walks straight ahead to a faded white circle with numbers (the remains of a sundial, she thinks), and picks up Willie's phone.

"Bravo," a familiar voice calls from behind and to her right. And there's Gary Jones, hatless, sitting on an upturned log.

"Where's Willie," Tonya demands.

"Safe." Gary's pale eyes are glittery, his face as slick and white as a dead flounder's belly. Tonya's stomach turns. "Aren't you happy to see me? I saved your son from the kidnapper. When I saw your husband's boyfriend toss the roadkill over your fence, I knew something was up. I waited and followed—"

Tonya cuts him off. "Where. Is. Willie."

"Jack doesn't want you to know that he and Duwayne are lovers."

Tonya blinks at the subject change. "What? When'd you speak to Jack?"

Gary gestures with his left hand. His other one's on the gun in his lap. A blond man lies on the ground to Gary's left, silenced and immobilized by a hundred wraps of duct-tape. A chrome motorcycle headlight gleams from the bushes.

"Now, Jack and Duwayne," Gary continues, "who I heard introduce himself to you on your doorstep with my way-cool bionic-ear listening device, want to open a motorcycle shop together. But what Jack didn't tell you is that they dream of living together above it in domestic

29

harmony. *That* was an interesting conversation. Jack really shouldn't talk on his phone when he's outside. Now, Jack and Duwayne, they must need money, right? Which you have plenty of, since the accident, right? See where I'm going with this?" Gary hums a few bars of a familiar tune. "I think it's about time for a pitching change, don't you, Tonya?"

"Jack would never do anything to hurt Willie," Tonya says.

"Oh, come on, Tonya," Gary says. "What more evidence do you need? Didn't you see Duwayne in his car? Didn't you see the bolt-cutters? I had to run like the dickens to beat him back to the car. He put Willie in the trunk, can you imagine? Duwayne sure was surprised to hear my voice from the back seat. Sorry about your lover, Jack. I had to shoot him to save your son. And now it's your turn. All together now, 'Na Na Hey Hey Kiss Him Goodbye'."

"Wait!" Tonya steps forward. "I don't want Willie to see."

Gary waves his right hand. "He can't see anything from—"

Willie's voice rings clearly through the trees. "I'm getting away, Mommy!"

"What the—" Gary jumps up. The gun begins to slide. "He can talk?"

Tonya dives for the gun. Gary knocks her away. She grabs his leg. He grabs the gun. She cries, "No!" Gary laughs and aims the gun at Jack's head. A flying missile named Ray tackles Gary from behind and proceeds to punch his lights out. Tonya gets in a couple of kicks. Jack moans encouragement from his prison of tape.

*****

Tonya shares a table outside an Ancient City coffee shop with Jack. It's Thursday. He's in cut-off jeans, just out of the hospital, bandaged and limping from the bullet wound he received when he met Gary at the old campground before Tonya arrived. The kids are in school. Tonya has a sub. Butterscotch rests her head on Jack's lap getting therapy pets.

"We need a family code word," Jack says.

"Agreed."

"How'd that guy get Willie's number anyway?" It was a text signed *love dad* that sent Willie and Ray to the men's room on Tuesday.

Tonya sighs. "When I got our phones, they gave me numbers in sequence."

"You gonna fix that?"

"Done."

A dishy Black man (high top fade, neat goatee, dimples) sits across from Tonya. Jack performs the introductions. Tonya doesn't ask to see his driver's license. She's fighting a new impulse not to trust. He's the real Duwayne Washington. The fake Duwayne was an attendee at the same Halloween party. Another eavesdropper. Tonya sips her latte, waiting.

"I wanted to tell you," Jack says quietly, "but I didn't know how."

Tonya wants to say, you coulda used your words, but says instead, "Not my business."

"But it *is* your business," Jack says. "You're family. We're family. It's—"

"It's complicated," Duwayne says, patting Jack's hand.

"It doesn't have to be," Tonya says.

"Doesn't it?" Jack looks hopeful.

Tonya holds up a finger. "First, tell me who you're hiding out from."

When Jack hesitates, Duwayne says, "Go on, tell her."

"There's this guy from work—" Jack begins.

"His boss's wife's cousin," Duwayne says, eyes dancing.

"He wants to sell me life insurance."

"Have you tried saying no?"

"Well, not in so many words."

Tonya shakes her head. "It's one word, Jack. Listen, I have to go meet Willie's bus."

Acting like it's not *the* question of the day, Jack asks, "Can we watch Willie while you go to Mia's game?"

"If y'all can be there by three-fifteen. Game's across town today."

"Not me, man," Duwayne says, holding up his palms. "I got to work. Sorry."

Tonya turns to Jack. "You riding with me then?"

"To an Airbnb?" Jack sounds like a child who's lost his favorite toy.

"Wherever you want," Tonya says, rolling her eyes at Duwayne.

Duwayne laughs delightedly. "I'll get his crutches."

*****

Tonya sits by herself on the bleachers. It's the third inning. The other team is winning by six runs. Mia's team better step it up. Tonya keeps checking her phone. It was hard leaving Willie home with Jack. But it was right.

Someone sits close to her. It's Ray. Surprised, Tonya signs a happy greeting. Ray doesn't sign anything back. She looks into his eyes for the reason, but he turns away to watch the game. When he reaches for her hand, she smiles. Words aren't everything.

The Rapper
The Jaggerz

The Rapper is a song by the Jaggerz,
written by band member Donnie Iris.
Originally released as a single, it reached #2
on the *Billboard* singles chart, held off the #1 slot by
Simon & Garfunkel's *Bridge Over Troubled Water*.
On March 20, 1970, it reached #1 on the
Record World singles chart.
Later that year, it was certified Gold by the RIAA
for selling over a million copies.

The Rapper
Josh Pachter

The slide projected onto the screen that hung above the back of the stage read:

WELCOME TO COMM 314
(INTERPERSONAL COMMUNICATION).
SIT NEXT TO SOMEONE YOU DON'T KNOW,
PUT AWAY YOUR ELECTRONICS,
AND TRY CONVERSING UNTIL I ARRIVE.
PROFESSOR DONALD I. RAPPAPORT

The students trickling into the auditorium in Slippery Rock University's Eisenberg Classroom Building that afternoon read the message and looked at each other in confusion, uncertain whether or not to take its instructions seriously.

Some didn't, either chattering with their friends or sitting hunched over their iPhones, scrolling through their TikTok feeds, their earbuds isolating them from the world around them.

Others, though—a few at first, more as the hands of the clock on the wall crept closer to 2 PM—laughed nervously at the words on the screen but came close to obeying them, sitting not quite *next* to a stranger but leaving one empty seat between them and leaning across it to offer self-conscious introductions.

"I'm Allie George," a blond co-ed in high-rise white chinos and a pale-blue sweater set whispered to the girl two places to her left, a girl who might almost have been her older sister except for her outfit and the color and length of her hair. "Have you heard anything about *him*"—she pointed with her chin at the unoccupied podium on the stage— "other than the glop on Rate My Professors?"

"Bonny Faiella," her almost-twin, who was wearing shorts and a yellow crop top despite the fall-semester Pennsylvania chill, said shyly. "My roommate had him for 217 last spring."

"What's 217?"

"Intercultural. You ask me, *that* ought to be the three-hundred-level course, and interpersonal should be two-hundred, but whatever. She says they call him the Rapper."

The girl sitting directly behind the empty chair that separated them leaned forward and rested her arms on its seatback. Her skin was chestnut, almost glowing under the fluorescent lights of the auditorium, and she was more appropriately dressed for the weather in gray sweatpants and a *Don't Knock the Rock* sweatshirt. "The Rapper?" she said. "*Please* tell me he doesn't actually *rap* his lectures!"

Bonny giggled. "Not *that* kind of rapper. He's a white guy. Anyway, he should be here any second and—"

"So? I mean, Eminem? The Beastie Boys? Machine Gun Kelley? White guys can rap."

"Still," Bonny said, "this one doesn't. Not like that, not according to my—"

"So what's his thing, then? I'm Kendra Koodrich, by the way. Do you mind?" She clambered over the empty seat without waiting for a response and snuggled in between the other two girls. Their three heads—Allie's crowned with long straight hair the color of cornsilk, Bonny's auburn mane shoulder-length and curly, Kendra's tight black microbraids elongating her face and drawing attention to her fine features—were close together, and Bonny Faiella was about to answer the question when the door at the back of the theater banged open and Donald I. Rappaport strolled in, a calfskin satchel slung over his shoulder.

He was a tallish man, a bit over six feet, forty-something, with a shaggy haircut beginning to go gray and a salt-and-pepper goatee. He wore distressed jeans and a chocolate-brown corduroy sports jacket with honest-to-God leather patches on the elbows. His eyes were a light blue behind steel half-frame glasses, and a hint of pipe tobacco trailed behind him as he came down the auditorium's center aisle and mounted the four wooden steps to plant himself behind the waist-high wooden podium with the Slippery Rock seal glued to its front.

"Welcome to COMM 314," he announced, the microphone attached to the podium amplifying his words and flinging them out across his audience of almost a hundred Strategic Communication and Media majors.

"After class," Bonny Faiella whispered, pulling a spiral-bound notebook from her backpack and flipping it open. "Boozers. We'll talk then."

*****

"That man has an ego the size of Dispirito Field," Allie said, stripping the paper from a straw and dunking it into a tall glass of unsweetened iced tea.

They were clustered around a Formica table in the Boozel Dining Hall, across the north end of the campus's Central Loop from the Vincent Science Center. It was 4:40 in the afternoon, too early for dinner, so the three co-eds had swiped in and grabbed drinks—plus a cupcake for Bonny, who was feeling serotonin-challenged and in need of a sugar hit.

"So let's hear it," Kendra said. "What did your roommate tell you about him?"

Bonny patted frosting from her lips with a paper napkin. "He's like the Notorious P.I.G.," she confided. "Teaches two classes a term and picks out one pet from each of them to groom. His wife *divorced* him, he says. He never gets to see his *kids*. He's *lonely*. He needs a 'companion,' a girl he can *talk* to."

"Talk to," Allie echoed. "I'm sure."

"First he meets with you in his office," Bonny went on, warming to the gossip. "Then eventually he suggests you come up to his place for some coffee or tea or whatever—except once you *get* there, he busts out the Jägerbombs, and then he's got you where he wants you."

"Sick," Kendra breathed. "Why doesn't somebody report his ass? I mean, hashtag Me Too the *fuck* out of him?"

"This is western Pennsylvania," Bonny said, "not Hollywood—not even Pittsburgh. And he's department chair. Everyone's scared to death of complaining about him—and even if they *did*, the administration would probably have his back."

"Somebody's got to *do* something," Allie said, "and I don't mean just rap the Rapper on the knuckles. Somebody's got to wrap him up but *good*."

*****

Though Allie George was the youngest of the three co-eds, she was also the most generously endowed, so when COMM 314 met for the second time, the following Monday, it was Allie who arrived at the Eisenberg auditorium early enough to snag a seat in the middle of the front row, just a few feet from the stage. She was wearing a tight black miniskirt and a V-necked cashmere sweater that, assisted by a push-up bra she'd Amazon Primed, further accentuated her cleavage.

When Donald Rappaport took his place behind the podium, arrayed once again in denim and corduroy, there was no way he could miss the display she put on for his benefit, and Bonny and Kendra later reported that, though they were seated several rows further back, they could see the professor's eyes widen with appreciation behind the lenses of his spectacles.

For the hour and a half of the day's lecture—which dealt with the difference between self-image and self-concept and the important role each plays in the perception process—the Rapper spoke directly to Allie and ignored the other students' occasional raised hands. For all practical purposes, it was as if the two of them were the only living human beings in the room.

As the session wound up, Rappaport made a point of announcing that he would be holding an office hour immediately after class, and then every Wednesday and Friday morning from eleven to noon. "If you have anything you'd like to discuss with me," he said, and then—gazing straight into Allie's big blue eyes—meaningfully added, "anything at all, please do come up to 213D and see me."

*****

But Kendra had learned about delayed gratification in her psych seminar, and once she explained the concept to Allie and Bonny the girls agreed it would be best to make the Rapper wait.

It was Friday morning when Allie showed up at Rappaport's office. She was dressed demurely in loose-fitting linen slacks and a silk blouse buttoned up to her throat—more delayed gratification—but strategically positioned wads of toilet paper in her bra assured that his attention would be drawn from her eyes to the promise of her pastures of plenty below.

"Ah," the professor said, looking up from a copy of the *Post-Gazette* folded open to the sports section, "you're in interpersonal, front row center. Miss—?"

"George," she said. "Allie."

"Allie." He stretched the word out in a way that made it sound almost dirty. "Come in, sweetheart, have a seat. What can I do for you?"

"I was hoping you could help me pick a topic for my term project," Allie said, which was a lie. She'd already chosen a topic and completed about half of the necessary research, but there was no need for *him* to know that.

*****

This first meeting lasted about fifteen minutes and would have gone on longer, but by then a line of students—more females than males—had collected outside Rappaport's office door, and he grudgingly suggested that Allie come back another time to continue their conversation.

She did, the following Wednesday, and then again on the Friday, each time dressed a bit more provocatively. It was during their third meeting that he proposed she visit him at his home, where they could talk at greater length without interruption. She feigned embarrassment at the suggestion and declined it primly, but he repeated it during her fourth visit and again the next time, and at that point she decided she'd delayed as long as was prudent and agreed.

*****

Donald Rappaport's two-bedroom ranch was just off campus at the corner of Maple and East Cooper, a seven-minute stroll from Allie's dorm room in Rhoads Hall. She rang his doorbell at seven that Thursday evening, wearing a pink tube top that bared her midriff and left little to the imagination, sandals, and a white denim skirt so short it would have gotten her sent home from high school if not suspended.

Rappaport welcomed her with exaggerated gallantry—barefooted, in tan chinos and a black T-shirt that showed off his toned biceps and triceps—and led her into a wood-paneled living room that reminded Allie of her grandfather's den in Grove City. She didn't recognize the melody emanating from the box speakers in the corners of the room but figured from the saxophone it was probably jazz. *Horny music*, she thought. *Perfect.*

She settled onto a sofa upholstered in a fabric she thought might be called something like *velour*, slipped out of her sandals, and folded her long bare legs beneath her. There was a ficus in a ceramic planter on the carpet beside the arm of the sofa she leaned against, a table bearing a shaded lamp next to the sofa's other end, a glass-topped coffee table holding a spotless ashtray and a squat four-wick candle that tinged the air with the smell of jasmine.

"Can I offer you something to drink?" the professor asked. "Before we get started?"

"Can I have a pop?" Allie said. "Coke Zero, if you have it, or else anything's fine."

"I'll have a look," he said, and disappeared into the kitchen.

When he returned a few minutes later, he was carrying a tray that held two pint glasses, two shot glasses, a blocky dark-green bottle, and two open cans of Red Bull.

"I thought I had some Cokes in the fridge," he apologized, "but I guess I'm out. Have you ever tried a Jägerbomb?"

Allie frowned. "A what? I don't really drink, Professor. I'm—"

"Donnie," he said. "You can call me professor on campus, but here in my home, how about making it Donnie?"

"All right," she said uncertainly.

"All right?" he repeated, tilting his head to one side.

"All right, *Donnie*," she corrected herself.

He set the tray on the coffee table and pulled up an armchair. Then, like a chemist in an ATS Hall lab, he poured Red Bull from one of the cans into a pint glass, opened the green bottle and filled a shot glass with Jägermeister, dropped the shot glass into the fizzy yellow-brown high-energy drink. He pushed the glass across the coffee table toward Allie and built one for himself, this time pouring from the other can of Red Bull.

"Cheers," he said, and reached to click the table lamp's three-way bulb down to its lowest level of illumination. When he leaned back in his chair, he saw that her glass was almost empty, and she was spluttering as if she'd swallowed a live earthworm on a dare.

"My, my," he said, "you're a thirsty little minx. Let me fix you another one."

*****

Twenty minutes later, the professor had moved from his armchair to sit beside Allie on the sofa and was pretending to be interested in her explanation of the difficulty she claimed to be having in narrowing the focus of her term project.

"The *real* problem," she said, and then she cut herself off in the middle of the sentence and stretched like a cat and yawned, shifting her legs enough to afford him just a glimpse of the white cotton of her panties. "Gosh, I'm so *tired*," she sighed. "It's weird—I got plenty of sleep last night."

"What you need," he said, "is one more Jägerbomb, but then I am cutting you off, young lady. I can't have you getting drunk on me. How would *that* look?"

He put the drink together. "I'll be back in a second," he said. "I just want to change into something a little more comfortable."

When he came out of his bedroom, he was wearing a patterned kimono belted around his waist, and the girl was sound asleep on the couch.

"Allie?" he said, sitting close beside her. "Allie?"

There was no response. The tops of her breasts rose and fell as she breathed in and out. Rappaport lowered his head to within a few inches of her chest and could just make out a faint snoring above the drone of his stereo. His latest conquest wore a tiny gold cross on a chain around her neck, he noticed, and he pinched it between his thumb and forefinger and tugged it gently. She didn't react.

He licked his lips and slid his hand inside the scoop neck of her tube top, cupped one young breast in his palm and eased it free of its restraint. He leaned closer and ran his tongue slowly across the nipple, the tang of her perfume exciting him.

"Oh, yes," he murmured. He stood and unknotted the belt at his waist and shrugged out of his kimono, which puddled on the carpet at his feet, leaving him completely naked, his terrible swift sword erect and eager for action.

"Let the games begin," he whispered.

And then Allie opened one eye and winked up at him. "Peekaboo," she said. "There's a game for ya."

He jerked back as if her skin had erupted into flame. "You—how are you awake? There was enough Rohypnol in those drinks to—"

She sat up and readjusted her tube top, putting her breast back where it belonged. "I didn't actually *drink* your drinks, Professor. I'm not twenty-one—I'd be breaking the law if I drank them. I hope I didn't kill your ficus."

"I—I—"

"You—you, on the other hand, *have* been breaking the law against supplying alcohol to a minor, which carries a *minimum* penalty of a thousand-dollar fine in this state. You really ought to ask for ID the next time you try to roofie a girl. Except I don't think there's ever going to *be* a next time."

Rappaport seemed at last to notice that he was nude, and he snatched up his kimono and hurried into it. "Your word against mine," he said, attempting to muster his dignity and salvage the situation. "And even if they believe yours, what's a thousand dollars to me? Maybe three days of my salary?"

"Oh, I think you're going to wind up losing more than a few days' pay, Professor. You just assaulted me, and I'm only seventeen years old."

"Sevent—but you're in a junior-level course!"

"I know, right? My IQ is like a hundred and sixty-something, and I skipped a couple of grades in elementary school and graduated way early."

A nasty smile crossed the professor's face. "Still, the age of consent in Pennsylvania is *sixteen*, so you're—"

Allie's smile outnastied Rappaport's. "Not so fast, Donnie. The Commonwealth recognizes that power imbalances—like teacher and student, for example—make consent impossible, regardless of age. I think what you did to me is gonna count as felony statutory sexual assault."

A bead of sweat trickled down the side of the man's face. "Still," he said uneasily, "your word against mine."

"Oh?" she said sweetly. "You think?"

And Kendra Koodrich stood up from her hiding place behind the professor's leather recliner and Bonny Faiella, emerged from the shadows of the hallway that connected the living room to the house's front door. Each of them was holding a cellphone in steady hands, and the phones were pointing directly at him.

"I don't think you've met my friends Kendra and Bonny," Allie said, stripping away the professor's last straw, "although they're taking COMM 314 with me. I let them in earlier, while you were in the kitchen, and they've been videotaping ever since. You got it all, girls?"

"Every disgusting moment," said Bonny. "Including a nice shot of him with his old-man dick all flopping around after he touched your boob."

"I already posted it to TikTok," added Kendra. "Complete with his name."

Professor Rappaport stood there in his patterned kimono, blinking impotently. "Who *are* you three?" he demanded, though now the bravado in his voice was clearly shaken. "What are you after?"

Their combined smiles appreciably increased the wattage of the room's subdued lighting.

"What are we after?" Allie echoed. "Well, you gotta face reality, Prof: we have trapped you, and we are gonna sock it *to* ya."

And Bonny Faiella, thinking about her roommate and all the other girls the Rapper had gotten away with abusing, answered his first question. "Trap, trap, trap," she chanted, grinning widely. "They call us the Trappers."

Seasons in the Sun
Terry Jacks

Seasons in the Sun is an English-language adaptation of the Jacques Brel 1961 song *Le Moribond* (*The Dying Man*) with the lyrics being rewritten in 1963 by American singer-poet Rod McKuen.

Canadian singer Terry Jacks released his version as a single in 1973 on his own label, Goldfish Records. On March 2, 1974, the song began a three-week run at #1 on the *Hot 100* and remained in the top 40 until almost Memorial Day weekend. *Billboard* ranked it as the number two song for 1974.

It was certified Gold by the RIAA in 1970 for selling over a million copies.

It's Hard to Die

J. M. Taylor

Jean barely felt the blade slice into his side. Just saw his friend Emil's face, an inch from his own. The look of hatred told him, though, that this was a farewell to everything they had shared. Then Jean felt the press of Emil's fist on his abdomen, savagely twisting the knife. Finally, a wave of heat burst from the epicenter of the wound and he knew he was going to die. It wouldn't be hard, but he wondered desperately what it could be for.

There must have been a slight he'd done, but for the life of him—and surely it was—he couldn't imagine what it was.

Sure, Emil was known for being hot-headed. Remember that time in primary school, when the two of them had tested each other all week for the spelling bee? The prize was a shiny medal on a tricolor ribbon. Word after word, Emil had been the better of the two. When it came time to compete in class, it became obvious that they had put more study time in than any of their friends. It took only two rounds to reduce the field to four, and Jean was certain that most of the class had screwed up purposefully just to avoid the hell of standing in front of the room.

But Jean and Emil and the two other girls battled it out until first Michelle, then Françoise sat down, furious to have lost the medal. The rest of the class stared out the window, some falling asleep, while the boys droned through one word after another. Only the last two girls showed any interest, but later Jean would wonder if it had anything to do with words.

The teacher had run through the entire list, so she pulled a dictionary from her shelf, flipped madly through the pages, and lobbed a pair of college-level words at them. Jean got through, simply by luck, and Emil missed by a single silent letter. Jean turned to shake his friend's hand, but Emil refused to take it, a shocking betrayal that perked up the interest of their classmates. Inevitably, it got taken care of after school, on the hill that rose behind the bleachers, where a taunting circle cheered while Emil bloodied Jean's nose, ruining the tricolor ribbon pinned to his chest.

Later, Emil tried to make it up by painstakingly drawing a picture of the medal, and Jean taped it to his wall. When they were in high school, sneaking a joint in Jean's bedroom, and blowing the smoke out the window, they would laugh about it, but Jean always saw a hint of resentment burning in Emil's eyes.

So as the wave of heat dissipated, to be replaced by a thousand different pains, Jean knew that there must have been some trigger for this madness. Surely Emil would recognize his mistake, realize that Jean was and always had been his loyal friend. Yes, Emil would pull out the blade, press something against the wound, and get Jean to the hospital. In the meantime, though, his knees grew unsteady, and he put his hand on Emil's shoulder to steady himself, as he'd done a hundred times or more since childhood.

And he'd needed that support, growing up. It wasn't the blood on the spelling medal that had bothered Jean's father, but the fact that he'd won it in the first place. Spelling, stories, history—none of that taught you how to treat a blight on your vines, got you through the backbreaking work of a grape harvest, or even how to keep the vats sterilized between batches. Hefting crates from dawn to whenever gave little time for reading, and the fact that Jean could lose himself in a poem when he should have been pruning along the rows or hefting hoses in the winery drove him to madness. No, it wasn't the blood, which stained just as spilled wine did. It was the fact that he'd won it in the first place. For Georges, school was nothing more than a way station on the way to work, and Jean had never boarded the next train.

When he was young, Jean's school success had been tolerated, and the boy was never sure why his father didn't do more than raise a glass half-heartedly at supper for his being at the head of the class. But as he got older, Jean saw the truth lurking in those sips like click beetles in spring blossoms: Georges was resentful of his son's intelligence. The winery was barely holding on, and it was because Georges had not finished school when he inherited the business from his own father. Because he couldn't read well enough and had only basic science schooling, he couldn't compete with the modernized methods of the industry. At first, he thought that being a traditional *vigneron*, using the ancient methods, would see him through. But time and time again he'd been cheated by a crafty fox of a *négociant* who would buy up his harvests for less than what he paid other growers, and whose trained chemists would transform his mediocre grapes into award-winning vintages.

When he was ten, Jean had promised his father he would grow up and become a lawyer to help save the vineyard, but Georges had only sneered and uncorked another bottle, the third of the night. "What do you know of law?" he said. "It was a lawyer who took your mother from me, a lawyer who said my brother should inherit the other half of the vineyard, even though he plowed it all under to build those God-awful cottages and sell them to foreigners to look over my work for their romantic holidays. Bah to your lawyers, Jean." He punctuated the rant by hurling the full bottle at the wall, where it shattered, leaving Jean to pick up the shards of green glass. The stain was never cleaned up.

He wished now that he could have just one more moment with his father, who this very moment probably sat at the wooden table, uncorking another bottle, wondering what went wrong with his son. Neither of them would ever know.

It was Michelle, the spelling runner-up, who noticed the blood on the back of Jean's neck the next day at school, where a piece of the bottle had ricocheted and stuck in the flesh. Sitting behind him, she saw the trickle seeping into his shirt collar. At lunch Emil let Jean grip his arm while she used a pin to pry it loose. Her best friend, Françoise, stood by, fascinated to see both the blood and Michelle's willingness to persevere as the shiny splinter held on to its place. When it finally slid out, she held it up for Jean to see. The green and red reminded him too much of the original crash, and he would have fainted then and there, even in front of the girls, if Emil hadn't steadied him.

He almost laughed to think how little that first sticking was. How painless, until Michelle had spotted it. But now the blood was pouring out, onto Emil's fist, and the one image that Jean remembered was the rose of wine on the kitchen wall that still confronted his father when he entered the kitchen each morning. How much would this gushing stain the carpet beneath him?

After that schoolyard surgery, the four of them became fast friends, held together by blood and books. Even in *collège*, they were reading Camus. In the woods they smoked and drank stolen wine, affecting existentialist poses that brought each of them detention at school and, for Jean, beatings at home. Emil, whose parents were rarely home, when they could leave him in the care of servants, yearned for any attention, even a slap. They took out their adolescent frustrations by beating on the younger kids, swaggering through the corridors. They maddened their teachers by continuing to get top marks, even when they were visibly hungover and their teachers wondered if and how they would speak to the parents.

Their little gang came to be known as "The Four Seasons." Françoise was fresh as spring, beautiful, but easily led, the innocent of the group. Michelle was cool and mature, as practical as autumn. Emil, ever tempestuous, was winter, but by all accounts, Jean was summer with his radiant mind and good looks, smoothing things over after one of Emil's outbursts. They wore their school uniforms according to their own inimitable fashion, and no one questioned their status in the schools. Students feared and worshipped them, teachers, to their humiliation, deferred to their authority.

As they moved on to the *lycée*, they discovered Collete and Anaïs

Nin. Knees held close to hide their exhilaration, they read passages aloud that made them shiver first with confusion, then with curiosity. The first few times, the boys stole behind clumps of rock or thick trees to relieve themselves. Later, it became a group project. Michelle used a cheap lipstick to emulate the Brazilian dancer in "The Hungarian Adventurer." She practiced some of the character's other feats as well.

Once, when Françoise bit too hard on his lip, Emil had slapped her so hard it left a mark. She ran ran off in tears, and Michelle left Jean unsatisfied to follow her. Emil, too, fell to the ground crying, and for two weeks, they never returned to their forest retreat. But Jean was so solicitous and apologetic to Michelle, bringing her a bouquet of roses every day for a week, that eventually they resumed their reading circle. The first time they fully committed to enacting the events on the page, it was Jean and Françoise who fumbled together behind an oak. But the four were so close, on any given summer afternoon it was a matter of who sat where that decided the pairs.

So many memories, pouring out with each slowing beat. The dregs of his life, and for what? Surely Emil would say something, but he watched as Jean gasped to ask why, and uttered not a word.

When they were sixteen, Jean was supposed to be helping with the grape harvest. Furious that he'd been left short-handed, Georges stomped through the house looking for the malingerer. He found Jean and Françoise tangled in the sheets of his bed, the sharp scent of marijuana flooding the room, practically wilting the corners of the crayon medal that still clung to the wall. Ignoring the screams of the girl who wrapped herself in the duvet, Georges dragged his son from the bed by his neck, spitting with fury at the humiliation his behavior had brought to the family, to the winery, to the town. Françoise snuck out of the room at some point, leaving her clothes behind, and calling Michelle from the kitchen phone to rescue her. Michelle arrived on a bicycle, and by the time they had got Françoise home, the duvet was splattered with mud and grease and shredded by the spokes of the tires.

The next day, Jean kept his swagger in the halls, despite not being able to see through one swollen eye. His careless smile put others at ease, until they barely noticed the purpling bruise, and began to think of it as nothing more than a passing cloud on a summer's day.

But the latest cloud darkened his eyes as the rush of blood left his vision blurred. His ears rang. Somewhere far away he heard a scream. Was it Michelle? She was supposed to be out tonight. Maybe she had come back early? Theirs had not been the easiest of marriages. She always came back to him, eventually.

Emil pulled the knife from his gut. Another explosion of pain ripped through his body. His legs gave way and he dropped to his knees. The shock woke him briefly and he looked first at Emil's stony face, then around the room in search of that continuing scream. Yes, Michelle was standing there. But she remained immobile, still as marble with a neutral expression on her face, never the one to be bothered by blood. It wasn't her that made that dreadful noise. Behind her, the darkened window glowed with the light of a crescent moon. A single star shone in its embrace.

The Seasons were dispersed upon graduation, each going their separate ways. Emil, with his father's fortune, decamped to Oxford, and when he was thrown out, he crossed the Atlantic to take Harvard by storm. Françoise studied architecture, while Michelle was determined to become a doctor. Jean, every bit as capable, remained in the vineyard, weathering his father's progressively pathetic ravings, trying his best to make a dying concern turn a profit. But during school breaks, they would all come together again, with tales of wild adventures with other boys and girls, that always ended with vows that such dalliances were mere games to pass the time.

In his lucid moments, Georges tried to pass on the vocation of viniculture to his son, but to Jean, it was simply repetitive tasks, with no joy to be found. He tried to find satisfaction in the work, but instead, was horrified to be following the same path as his father: looking at the bottoms of too many bottles, finding a moment of pleasure in too many women, wishing all of them were one of his childhood friends.

Ironically, it was Emil who had set him straight. The first one home for a holiday in his last year in the US, he had found Jean carousing in the street outside a bistro, and carried him home.

"It's time to grow up," Emil said. "Get married, raise a family."

"Who would have me, a drunken, failed farmer who cares nothing for his crops?"

Emil helped him into the house, and sat him at the table, with his back to the unfaded starburst of wine on the wall.

"I know plenty. But truly, there are only two for us."

Jean sighed and dropped his head in his hands. "But how to choose? We've all been so close. Both Françoise and Michelle will be home tomorrow."

"Yes," Emil agreed. "How? I think I know a way."

The next day, Emil appeared in the vat building, as Jean was uncorking a bottle to celebrate the setting of the sun.

"Put that aside," he said. "We'll be seeing our other halves tonight. It's time to decide."

"How?"

"Here is the answer." He held up a pair of flowers, roses white and red. "Let you be the red, and I shall be the white. This evening, when we meet the other seasons at the bistro, we lay them out. We do not tell them anything, but the one who chooses each of our colors, shall be our wife."

They agreed. And when Michelle and Françoise appeared at the bistro, arm in arm, Jean had to admit to himself that he was gratified, watching them reach for a flower, that Michelle had taken the red. Of course she had, Michelle who had always been fascinated with blood, whose clinical practicality would rein in his excesses. But Jean couldn't help but notice the jealousy in Emil's eyes, as he realized he would be left with the spring flower Françoise. Her beauty and poise were unsurpassed, but Michelle's adventurousness would never be matched.

It was that adventurousness that Michelle displayed now. As Jean dropped to his knees, she studied him like a lab experiment. He was not one of her patients. He was her husband, but he knew he had been a disappointment, knew that she had more than once left him passed out, and found satisfaction in the arms of other men. There was nothing he could do about that now, except to say, "Goodbye, Michelle."

The heat had given way to a deathly chill. Emil stepped back, already showing the inevitable regret that came with his outbursts. As Jean swayed on his knees, desperately trying to hold the last gouts of blood in the wound, he discovered that the screaming was the sound of the approaching police car. Who had called so quickly, and why did these two only watch? It was hard to die by oneself, surrounded by the two he loved...no the three he loved the most.

Françoise stepped into the house, her hands at her mouth. "What have you done?" she said to her husband, as the police drew closer. "You stupid man, what have you done?" Her voice had the tinny sound of rehearsal as if she had been preparing all along to say the words.

"You told me you had a lover," Emil said to his wife, tears in his voice. "So I checked your mobile. Time and again, you came here. I couldn't allow him to have you and Michelle both."

Jean slumped to the floor. The knife dropped next to him. Then Emil was holding him, pressing his hand to the wound. "My trusted friend," Jean whispered. He tried to shake his head. *No,* he meant to say. *That wasn't true.*

The room was dark, and his vision was nearly gone. The last thing he clearly saw was that Françoise had reached out for Michelle's hand. Michelle, who still watched without comment. He wasn't sure, but it seemed, in his sporadic clarity, that the two clung to each other like lovers.

The police had arrived, and Jean knew he had only moments to say goodbye. Emil was weeping but it was Michelle and Françoise that held his last seconds of attention. He heard his wife whisper, "You did well, *ma chérie.*"

How could the police know of this petty tragedy, unless they had been forewarned? Who could have known that Emil would react with such violence? Who would know that in a single moment, both men's lives would be ended? Françoise had come here, it may be true, but since the time Georges had found them in his bed, they had never once slept together. Only now did he come to understand that these women, who had once reenacted with him and Emil the hedonistic scenes of Anaïs Nin in their woodland bower, these women who, when the boys crept off to relieve themselves, were free to relieve each other, and had all along been in love with each other. All along, he had seen only two possible pairings. Never had he imagined, there were more.

Only as he died, did Jean understand that lovely Spring and chilled Autumn had found a way to bypass the extremes of winter storms and summer sun and that the seasons were all gone.

Wildfire
Michael Murphey

Wildfire is a song written by Michael Martin Murphey & Larry Cansler. It was originally recorded by Murphey, who had yet to add his middle name to his recorded work, and appears on his 1975 album *Blue Sky – Night Thunder*.

Released in February 1975 as the album's lead single, it became Murphey's highest-charting pop hit in the United States. The song hit #2 in Cash Box,
and #3 on the Billboard Hot 100 in June 1975.

The single continued to sell, eventually receiving platinum certification from the RIAA for sales of over 2 million US copies. Members of the Western Writers of America chose it as one of the Top 100 Western songs of all time.

Wildfire
Christine Verstraete

Once Stella Thomas saw him, she knew the horse had to come home with her.

Black, sleek, and beautiful, the 16 hands-high stallion had strong, powerful legs and a thick mane that flowed like an inky waterfall. A young horse yet at maybe three or four years, she didn't know how he'd ended up on the auction block.

The reason didn't matter. She vowed to save him.

"You're safe now," she whispered, rubbing the velvety nose of the handsome stallion she'd already dubbed Wildfire. The horse nickered softly and pressed his head into her palm as if in thanks.

As the stallion was already broke and seemed docile enough, she had no trouble loading him into the trailer for the short ride to the riding arena and stables at Sunflower Farms. Luckily, her friend and stable owner Ginger had agreed to board the horse in exchange for Stella teaching therapeutic riding lessons for special needs children. She loved doing it anyway.

"What're you going to tell Mark?" Ginger asked, getting behind the wheel of the battered green Ford truck. "Didn't he say no more horses?"

"Nothing, absolutely nothing. You know how he is. He thinks my saving horses is a waste of time and money. I disagree, of course."

"You knew what he thought about horses when you married him."

"Fool I was. After two years, I'd hoped he'd come around once he saw what it meant to save them, especially when you started the special riding lessons. He knew I'd been in love with horses since my 4H days, but as he put it, 'time to grow up and get over it.'"

"They are a money-suck," Ginger added as she pulled the truck through the gate topped by a giant sunflower carving. "I know that."

"Hey, I'm cheap otherwise. I wear old jeans, boots, and holey denim jackets, not designer clothes. I don't get manicures, not that I couldn't use one. I trim my own hair. My money goes to the horses."

They pulled in close to the barn. Stella jumped out, opened the trailer, and led Wildfire down the ramp and into a stall that smelled to her like hopes and dreams under a layer of hay and manure. Good smells. The horse snorted and bobbed his head, settling in with no problem. She rubbed his silky flank and smiled as she filled the water tray and hung a new feed bag. Nope, no regrets.

A deep voice interrupted her musings. She turned to find Mark standing there, a scowl on his face as he rubbed a dirty spot off his pristine suit jacket. Make that one regret.

"Stella, what's this? I thought I said no more horses."

She raised an eyebrow and stared at him, wondering how she didn't see his controlling attitude before they'd married. It'd been there, in smaller doses then, but she'd been in love and took his snide remarks as concern instead.

"Mark, what're you doing here? I thought you didn't like coming to the stable."

He crossed his arms and looked around, his nose wrinkling at the assorted scents in the air. "I don't. You weren't home, so I figured you'd be here. You seem to prefer horsing around instead of taking care of responsibilities at your own house."

She let the accusations slide, ignoring his attempt to manipulate her and make her feel small. Not anymore.

They fell silent as Ginger entered the barn, her hands full of reins and bridles, which she hung on the rack of wall hooks without giving Mark a second glance.

"Stella, everything okay? We've got lessons starting in a half-hour."

"Everything's fine. I was telling Mark—"

He interrupted, his voice gruff. "Lessons, what lessons?"

"I'm teaching a few more lessons in exchange for room and board," Stella explained.

"I see." He glowered at her. "Then I guess I'll pick up some fast food for dinner. Again."

Stella saw how he clenched and unclenched his hands. She unconsciously rubbed her still-sore elbow from when he'd pushed her into the wall two days ago. As his temper tantrums increased and his aggression toward her grew, Stella knew she'd be better off going home late after he'd gone to sleep—or maybe not at all.

Not sure what to say, she carefully closed the stall door, resting her arm atop the wood frame as the horse dipped its head and blew his warm breath against her skin. She fought to stay calm and not show fear as Mark moved closer.

Stella subtly eased back a step as Ginger came over and hung a new bridle set on the wall, putting some space between her and Mark.

"Stella, I forgot to mention. Your last lesson doesn't end until nine, and there's a big storm coming. It might be best to stay over. I've got fresh chili and homemade cornbread for dinner. Mark, you're welcome to stay, too."

Mark's deepening frown told Stella he knew the argument was over, for now. He'd be sure to tell her what was what when she finally went home. Another reason not to.

"Huh? No, uh, no" he muttered. "I've got work to do. Stella, I'll see you later."

She finally released the breath she'd been holding as he stalked off. "Ginger, thank you."

Her friend stood still and gave her a stern look. "How long has this been going on? You know this kind of thing only gets worse."

"I know." Stella let out a long sigh. "He's always been short-tempered, but he seems to be getting worse."

"So, what are you going to do? I'm worried about you."

"I'm okay, honest." Stella exited the barn with her friend and entered the cozy kitchen, relishing the sweet scent of fresh-baked cornbread and the spicy smell of home-cooked chili.

Ginger dished out the chili topped with bits of sharp cheddar cheese and sour cream, and set the plate of cornbread on the table. "Listen, stay as long as you like. I mean it. I've got plenty of room. I just want you to be safe."

"You don't know how much that means to me." Stella glanced away, trying to hold back the tears that threatened to fall. "I've been seriously thinking of leaving him, but I wasn't sure what to do, or where I'd go. That makes it easier. Thank you."

"All right then. I can take you home tomorrow while he's at work to pick up your things. You have a joint bank account?"

Stella nodded.

"Then you better withdraw some money and set up a new account for yourself. I can lend you some cash if needed, but you don't want to be broke. Now eat while it's hot."

She took a bite, savoring the combination of sweetness with a kick. "Wow, Ginger, this is delicious. I used to not like chili. I would've changed my mind if I'd tasted yours."

"Well, thank you. You can't beat my chili, I always say. It's good stick-to-your-ribs food. Once we're done, I'll get you some clothes to sleep in. The bathroom's next to your room. There's an extra toothbrush and toiletries in the top drawer. You're welcome to come down and have a glass of wine, watch TV, or use my library. Don't feel bad if you'd rather turn in early. *Mi casa* is *su casa*."

"But what about the lessons? Shouldn't I go get the horse ready?"

Ginger's laughter filled the room. "Oh, sugar, you're not working tonight. I lied. I saw how things were going. I had to get rid of Mark somehow."

That got Stella laughing, too. "That was quick thinking."

"But it doesn't mean I'm letting you off easy," Ginger added. "We have a full schedule of lessons tomorrow. We'll start once we get back from your place and the bank."

"You bet," Stella said.

Her phone began ringing repeatedly later that night. After answering the first two calls peppered with angry threats, and lots of name-calling and swearing, Stella let the rest go to voice mail. They came every half-hour, then every hour. When her inbox filled, she dumped the calls without listening. She saved a few of the messages and forwarded some to Ginger as well for safekeeping.

*****

Two days later the irate messages finally stopped. The next time Stella answered her phone all she heard was heavy breathing. Then came the hang-ups.

That wasn't the worst of it. She didn't want to admit being uneasy, but mentioned it to Ginger after they'd finished the day's lessons.

"I didn't want to say anything, but I think someone was hanging around the barn."

Ginger's frown deepened. "I know we've had quite a few new people coming for the late lessons. Did they say or do anything? Threaten you? I'll make sure they're out on their ear."

"No, nothing like that. Just a funny feeling I had. I know you don't like people in the barn by themselves. I'd never seen this guy before but when I came back, he was gone. Maybe I'm just jumpy."

"No wonder, with all those calls you've been getting. I think it's time you contacted a lawyer and the sheriff. Put an end to the harassment."

"The calls have slowed down. I don't want to rile him up."

"Think about it," Ginger said. "In the meantime, I'm going to post some signs that no one is allowed in the barn without permission. I hate to change the locks and give out keys or codes on a need-to-know basis, but I will if necessary."

"I don't think you have to do that. I'll let you know if I see anyone suspicious."

"Okay then, I'll keep my eyes open, too, and tell the workers to do the same."

*****

Staying busy and throwing herself into her work made Stella forget about everything else. Wildfire turned out to be a good-natured and truly gentle horse. He was patient with the kids, and the young riders adored him. They seemed to be drawn to the horse and loved rubbing their small hands along his satiny coat.

Even Ginger was surprised to see the connection the animal had with the children, and agreed to let Stella try him out in a couple of lessons. "I can't believe someone would dump such a wonderful horse."

Stella smiled. "Me, too. But their loss was my gain."

"And mine," Ginger added and laughed. "I can see he's going to be a big draw around here."

The winds picked up and the skies turned an evil shade of gray by the time the last lesson ended. Stella eyed the threatening clouds and wondered how bad the storm would get. She shivered at the chill in the air.

"Brr, getting right nippy," Ginger observed. "Believe it or not, they're calling for an early snowstorm. Why don't you close everything up? I'll go finish dinner."

"Sure. I'll check the horses and lock the barn. I'll be in once I brush Wildfire and get him settled."

Stella made sure all the stall doors were locked and finished putting fresh hay in her horse's stall. She pressed her body next to his, the horsey smell and barn scents making her feel safe and content. Getting him had been one of the best decisions she'd ever made.

The horses whinnied nervously when something hit the front of the barn. "Easy, there, easy. It's only a storm. You're safe."

She dimmed the lights to calm the horses and went to grab her bag from the wall hook when she heard another thump at the front of the barn. Walking over, she saw the entrance door swinging back and forth. The rain grew heavier and turned to sleet, making it nearly impossible to see much outside.

The horses stomped in their stalls as the storm quickly bloomed into a squall. Stella fought to pull the door shut against the howling gusts. She'd finally managed to get it closed when she heard a scrape behind her and turned.

"Hey, what're you—"

The rest of her words got swallowed up in the roar of the storm.

*****

Twenty minutes later, Ginger peeked out the kitchen window for the third time, wondering how long Stella was going to take. The chicken was ready, and the potatoes already cooling. She'd have to reheat everything.

The bad weather had started to ease a bit, the darkest clouds moving out over the adjacent sunflower fields, the heads now hanging heavy with too early clods of ice and snow. Thinking she'd better see what was keeping her friend, Ginger pulled on the yellow rain slicker that she kept near the door and hurried out into the moonlit night. The air felt cool and clean. An owl gave a soft *hoo-hoo* in a nearby tree.

She headed down the gravel path, surprised to hear banging sounds, and noticed the front barn door had been left open. It swung back and forth, hitting the frame with a clunk. With an irritated sigh, she stepped into the barn, yanking the door shut behind her. She'd told Stella that the frame swelled sometimes and to pull the door hard in bad weather.

She walked into the dim interior, hearing only the snorts and snuffles of the horses in their stalls. As she turned the lights up higher, her anger faded. It had been a long day. Maybe Stella had fallen asleep in the horse's stall. It wouldn't be the first time she'd find the young woman sound asleep, her body nestled in the hay next to Wildfire.

But not this time.

The hairs on her neck prickled as she slowly approached the open door and found the stall empty. No horse, no rider.

"She couldn't have gone out riding now," Ginger muttered. "She knows these storms can start up without any warning."

Ginger rushed down the center aisle, checking the remaining stalls. All the other horses were safe, if not a little edgy.

She went down the left aisle, reaching out to rub the head of one of the saddle horses. "Easy, there, easy…"

The unease she'd felt slowly turned to disappointment, followed by a touch of anger. She'd told Stella not to ride when the weather was bad. No telling what a horse would do, or what would spook them. It was a good way to get hurt, or worse.

The rest of her musings stopped when she saw several small red spots on the hay-strewn floor. She leaned down, her alarm growing as she realized what she was looking at... blood.

Heart pounding, she followed the trail which changed into a long red line where the hay had been scraped aside as if something had been dragged.

"No," she whispered, her inner alarms clanging. "No, no."

Ginger followed the bloody path to the end of the aisle and gasped at the sight of a dark, viscous pool. Had Stella fallen and hurt herself?

Her eyes filled with tears as she followed the rest of the red streaks to the door. She opened it and saw nothing outside but clumps of ice and snow left over from the storm. Her hopes rose that maybe Stella had managed to stagger away and could still be helped.

Frantic, she grabbed the flashlight hanging on the side of the barn, turned it on, and shone it back and forth. She yelled and called, "Stella! Wildfire!" as she searched everywhere, even on the paths leading to the fields.

So far, she hadn't seen more blood or any other signs that Stella had fallen nearby, or that she had taken off on the horse. Where was she?

"Stella! Stella, can you hear me? Wildfire!"

She heard and saw nothing. Not even a hoofprint.

Her cries flew away in the burgeoning breeze. She brushed back the hair that whipped across her forehead, eyes wide as she surveyed the row upon row of sunflowers, her favorite blooms failing to bring the usual sense of joy or comfort.

Heart heavy, she turned to go in and call the sheriff when she realized she hadn't checked behind the barn. Her sense of dread grew as she spotted an unknown object lying in the grass. She edged closer, afraid of what she'd find, even more afraid of what it meant. It took only a few seconds for her to recognize the shovel from inside the barn, the end smeared with blood. So much blood.

She bit back a sob and ran inside to report the crime. The call made, she stood in the doorway and watched angry-looking clouds gathering. Rumblings and short flashes of lightning signaled the imminent return of the storm.

As she stared at the distant fields, Ginger thought she saw the black shape of a horse streak by. "Wildfire!" she yelled. "Wildfire!"

Her mind must be playing tricks on her.

*****

Days later, Ginger sat in the kitchen, her fingers tapping out a pattern on the table as she waited for news.

Someone knocked at the door. She opened it to a tall deputy, his expression somber, and braced herself for the worst.

"I'm sorry, but we found the body of a blonde-haired woman dressed in jeans and cowboy boots," he informed her. "She was lying in the weeds in an unplanted farm field down the road."

Ginger cleared her throat. "Yes, that sounds like her."

"We brought your friend Stella's husband Mark in for questioning but his lawyer claims he has a solid alibi for the time of the murder. We're waiting on DNA results and doing everything we can to solve this. I'm very sorry."

She nodded.

"Does she have any other family? If not, we'll ask you to come in for formal identification."

"There's no one else. I can do it."

"We'll let you know when."

Ginger watched him leave, her insides numb.

"Wait," she called. "Was... was she alone? Her horse..."

"No, sorry, we didn't find a horse," the deputy told her softly.

*****

A month later, Ginger continued to drive around the area hoping she might spot a black stallion grazing alone. She constantly checked her phone messages, praying someone responded to her ads offering a reward for the return of a lost black horse that answered to the name Wildfire.

The moon rose full and bright as she entered the barn, her fingers caressing the smooth surface of the gold plaque in her hand. She could think of no better tribute than putting up a visible reminder of the friend she had lost, killed by a jealous husband. The trial was set for early next year.

The engraved plaque read, *In Remembrance of My Friend Stella and Her Horse Wildfire, Kindred Souls.* She would hang the plaque on Wildfire's former stall later that evening in a dedication ceremony attended by friends and the other riders with their families.

With a sigh, Ginger stared into the distance, whispering a silent prayer that Stella's beautiful horse was safe and had somehow, somewhere, found a new home.

Glancing out at the now-harvested sunflower field, she listened to the whistle of the wind and swore she saw the dark shadow of a horse gallop past, but then it was gone…

STEREO
Intro 14
3:45

48 RPM
18-02646
ZSS 168355
℗ 1981 CBS Inc.

TOMMY TUTONE
867-5309/JENNY
A. Call - J. Keller- Taken From The Columbia
Lp "TOMMY TUTONE-2" ARC 37401
Produced by Chuck Plotkin
and Tutone-Keller

867-5309/Jenny
Tommy Tutone

867-5309/Jenny is a song written by Alex Call & Jim Keller, which was performed by Tommy Tutone. It was originally released as the first track on the album Tommy Tutone 2 in 1981 on Columbia Records. The song reached #4 on the US *Billboard Hot 100,* and #1 on the *Billboard Rock Top Tracks* chart in April 1982.

Like similar songs which quote telephone numbers, the song led to a spate of people dialing 867-5309 and asking for Jenny.

In October 2006, VH1 listed *867-5309/Jenny* as the 36th greatest song of the 1980s

Pigeon Talk

Sandra Murphy

I rolled over and up into what my mother called 'the you'll never get the hang of it, will you dear,' failed lotus position.

The sun was warm and comforting, tempered by a soft breeze. I was reminded of an old Irish prayer for the dead, 'may the road rise up to meet you, may the wind always be at your back, may the sun shine warm upon your face'. It seemed appropriate for today. Sun and breeze, two out of three, not bad. Maybe I could just stay here, forever. It seemed like a better idea than going, where exactly?

A brown and white marbled pigeon landed about six feet away. The bird walked its pigeon-toed walk a few feet closer, making soft coo noises with each step.

"Doesn't the gravel hurt your feet? It sure hurt mine." Sirens that minutes ago had been in the distance, were now blocks away. "I can't imagine why somebody would put gravel on a rooftop."

Several stories below, not sure how many, five or six at a guess, sirens faded as voices rose. I could hear the whoomp whoomp of a helicopter's approach. The pigeon bobbed its head at the noise. "It's about to get crazy." I squinted at the sky, the helicopter in sight, police department markings clear. "I think they're looking for me. Not sure if that's a good thing or bad."

The little bird walked to the edge of the roof, near the fire escape, and looked down, then back at me. With a slight bird style knee bend, it launched itself into the air and dropped out of sight. I closed my eyes against the too-bright sun.

A minute later, the iron door creaked open, followed by the crunch of footsteps.

I didn't move, didn't even turn my head. My hands remained on my knees, Zen-like, and I hoped in plain sight.

"Do you have a weapon?"

"No, is yours aimed at me? We're alone up here and I'm no threat to you."

"Good to know." He crunched closer. "Are you okay? You're bleeding."

"What? Oh, yeah. I fell, skidded a ways," I said. "This gravel is a pain to sit on, let me tell you. Running barefoot's no picnic either." I lifted my face to the sun to dry my tears, eyes still closed. "You got a name or should I just go with hey, you?"

"Officer Cooper, Charlie. Could you move farther back? You're making me right nervous."

"Why, Officer Cooper, Charlie, did you take a course in crisis intervention recently? That was textbook." I tried to roll the tension from my shoulders. It didn't budge, maybe settled in for life, short or long as that might be. I should take the situation more seriously. Smart ass is my default position under difficult circumstances. Cops don't always appreciate my sense of humor. Today would count as in the top three most stressful days of my life, but only if I could remember two others.

"Um, yes, ma'am, I did. You being too close to the edge would make me nervous no matter what. Plus, you're bleeding worse than just scrapes."

I heard the pop of a buckle unsnap. "Officer Cooper, Charlie? Are you reaching for your radio? You're going off-script. You should ask me my name, establish rapport." My mouth hadn't gotten the memo to show more respect.

He cleared his throat and said, "It's easier to talk to someone if you know their name. You know mine, what's yours?"

"I'm Jenny. Next question is do I want to talk to someone, a friend, family member, or a priest maybe? I do. I want Pete Lambert."

"Pete Lambert, like the Chief of Detectives?" Charlie was at a loss to understand. "You know him? I mean, you…"

"Look like a beat-up bag lady, all dirty, and probably smelly? Didn't they teach you not to go by appearances? Go ahead, use your radio but only to call for Pete."

"You ain't fixing to jump, are you?" He took a step closer.

"Stay back. If I was a jumper, I'd have been down on the sidewalk before you got up here." I started to laugh and couldn't stop. "That ship has sailed or maybe I should say, that pigeon has flown."

"Ma'am, Jenny, this is nothing to laugh about. A man's dead down on the sidewalk. Looks like maybe he was up here before he got down there. You know anything about that?"

I tried to turn my head but got no cooperation. The sun wasn't a comfort now, just too damn hot, the breeze only stirring up dust and the smell of exhaust. The hovering helicopter didn't help matters any.

"You're a nice man, Officer Cooper, Charlie. I like you." The roof was moving, like a tilt-a-whirl ride at the carnival, the one that always made me throw up cotton candy residue. "I feel kinda dizzy. Yeah, I know about that guy. I…"

The road didn't rise up to meet me but the rooftop and my face made a sudden acquaintance, gravel and all.

*****

"Hey, Bobby B! Okay if I put up another flyer? The last one disappeared." I held up the bright neon green paper. At his nod, I pinned it to the cork bulletin board. "You're the best, thanks."

> **Like long walks along the riverfront after dinner?**
> **Strolls through the park?**
> **Snuggles, popcorn, and TV time?**
> **Games, puzzles, and exploring new places?**
> **For a Good Time, call 867-5309**

That ought to get attention. I had three more coffee shops and a couple of lunch places to post flyers, maybe the Whole Foods bulletin board, too, if I had time. I wasn't about to rush today. Bobby B makes the best mochas and saves eclairs for me.

As usual, I brought my little laptop, sized more for a five-year-old's hands than my grownup fingers. I updated my Facebook page, posted and re-posted, deleted spam, and Instagrammed myself into a second éclair, just to keep my energy level high.

Josh stopped by my table to let me know the soup of the day for Wednesday would be corn chowder, my favorite, and he'd save me two bowls with half a dozen mini cheddar biscuits. Our schedules seem to be in sync. He's a nice guy, not datable for me, but good for a recap of news in the neighborhood and soup day insider information. Sue Ann rushed past, on her way to work. "Drinks, Friday happy hour?" I nodded. We always went to a non-chichi bar, no chrome, no weird drinks, just good conversation, the best appetizers, and no problem with guys who were only there to troll.

After the second éclair had met its fate and, to my disappointment, there were no more stashed or in the pastry case, I made my rounds to the other shops and Whole Foods. I circled back to Bobby B's to grab one more end-of-the-day coffee. It was time for me to get to work.

I rounded the corner and almost bumped into a delivery guy. "Hey, don't you deliver to Coffee Me? Didn't I see you there the other day?"

He nodded, "I'm at most of the shops once or twice a week. I deliver for Coffee Classics and Tea Time." He looked over my shoulder, prompting me to check what caught his attention. No one was there. He must be shy, didn't make direct eye contact.

"A black cargo van, huh? What is this, a cover for an FBI sting? In movies, they always use a van, like no one will notice." I laughed to make sure he didn't think I was serious.

"Yeah, and the fake sewer workers and guys on the telephone poles? So obvious."

"No logo? Which company do you drive for?"

"Self-employed."

"Me, too. I'd better get myself home and do some work."

"I need to get inside. Bobby B's running low on French roast."

"Can't have that! See you around." I enjoyed the not-quite-summer weather on my short walk home. From the walkway between Bobby B's and PrintManDo's Speedy Print Shop to the back of the building, then four businesses down, a left turn into the alleyway that runs behind my street, and I'm home. It makes Bobby B's way too convenient.

I live alone, a temporary condition, I hope. Of course, with my goofy non-schedule, it would take a flexible, special someone to put up with nights so late, they're considered morning by most people, poor things. That's why Bobby B orders two extra eclairs on days he knows I'll be in. I'd never manage to beat the morning rush. Of course, that rush is often my bedtime but out of courtesy for others, I don't inflict them with my 'need sleep, leave me alone' self at what I consider to be the crack of dawn.

My job title is freelancer which means my work schedule is varied. So are my paychecks. It's akin to walking a tightrope, survivable as long as you don't look down. With a Tuesday deadline, I needed to concentrate on an article for Apartment Living about pops of color for the kitchen. A controversial subject, color on the walls or the appliances? I looked around my own kitchen. A red toaster. Black and white tile on the walls. Yeah, not feeling it.

"You think you're so funny, how do you like this, Bill?" I leaned back in my chair, satisfied I'd shown him. "What are you doing? Nooo." But yes, Bill the Avatar used by Gin Rummy Gurus, had drawn the card I'd been waiting for, discarded a red king, and caught me with a handful of nothing but points. Research for my article titled *Keep Your Brain Active to Avoid Dementia* promised games would keep my mind limber. Bill, having no actual body, had the ability to be more flexible. Or he cheats. I sighed, dealt another hand, and hoped for three of a kind.

It took four more games but I beat Bill 456 to 74 so I was able to walk away a winner. Chalk one up for me! Chalk…

That word gave me just the idea I needed for the article. Chalkboard paint on two small areas, around the back door and the pantry, easy to do, easy to change. I suggested avocado mousse and lemon chiffon, trending colors, soft but not pastel, and certainly not a reminder of the 70s harvest gold and avocado. I'd advise bright colored chalk, something toward citrusy lime and orange maybe. Some days, I'm a genius.

I cut and pasted my notes, quotes, and suggestions into a semblance of order. Once I have the opening sentence, I'm good. It might not be a keeper but it's the starting pistol. I'd let the article simmer and polish it tomorrow, one day ahead of schedule. I settled down to a Netflix and microwave popcorn reward and gave Avatar Bill time to recover from his scorching defeat.

By the time I woke on Monday, I felt the need to see people. Live people who talk, not Bill. It was past the lunch rush, pre-after work business, so perfect for me. Loaded baked potato soup, extra cheese in lieu of bacon, a crusty dinner roll, and a strawberry banana smoothie sounded like a balanced meal to me. I could polish the article before the commuters arrived, use Bobby B's Wi-Fi to send it, and hope for an éclair or two as my reward.

Meal finished, no celebration éclair yet, I powered up to type. I'd hardly started to edit when I saw a familiar face. He approached my table and leaned in to ask a question. I nodded, closed the computer, and headed to Bobby B at the barista station. "Watch that for me? I'll be back in a few." He nodded and stashed it and my file folder under the counter and yelled, "Stan C, four shot iced, venti, four pump vanilla, six pump caramel, stevia, extra whip, and a cherry, one warmed cinnamon roll, side salad, no dressing, eat in." No dressing? Save calories where you can, I guess.

My plan to return in a few minutes? It didn't work out that way.

*****

I woke up in the dark before the dawn. The sun struggled to rise but didn't seem all that interested. I had the same feeling with a whopper of a headache banging around my brain. I reached for my phone, always on the nightstand, but it wasn't there.

In fact, the nightstand wasn't there.

I can be confused by the day of the week or the time of the day, but I've never misplaced furniture. I rolled to the other side of the bed. Not there either but a new surprise came to light. I was fully dressed. Minus shoes.

The sun had peeked over the shadows enough for me to see, so I stood and turned in a circle. Nothing was where I thought it should be.

Or maybe I was looking at it the wrong way. Maybe everything was where it was supposed to be.

I was the one out of place.

*****

"Bobby B's, how can we caffeinate you today? What? I can't hear you. No, still not. Hold on, move the phone away from your ear, I'm going to yell." Bobby put his hand over the phone and blasted the shop with a two-fingered shrill whistle. "Everybody, quiet!" All commotion stopped except for one baby who started to cry. Vanessa, who worked behind the pastry counter, grabbed a tray of nothing-allergenic-cookies, the baby, and Pied Pipered her way to the kid's play area.

"I'm back. What were you saying? No, not today. I'm not sure, it's hard to keep track of days. I go more by Mocha Monday, like that. Damn, no, you're right to be worried. Text me your digits. I'll ask around and get back to you. Yeah, right away."

Bobby B walked to the center of the room. "Has anybody seen Jenny today? Yesterday? That was her editor who called. She says Jenny wrote a rush article for her and emailed to say she'd send it Monday evening. Now it's Thursday morning, there's no article, and she hasn't been able to reach Jenny. Who's seen her, where, and when?"

Voices bounced off the walls and fell into an unintelligible mumble. "Quiet, please!" One of the customers stood. "No one can hear when everyone talks." She reached into her laptop case and pulled out paper, tape, and markers. "Now we need to know when each of us saw Jenny last. No one has seen her today. What about yesterday, Wednesday?"

No one spoke. "Tuesday? No? Then let's start farther back with

Saturday and work our way forward." People raised their hands for Saturday. One guy whispered, "Who the heck is she, putting herself in charge?"

"Emily, PTO president, K through 3." At the man's puzzled look, the woman explained, "Parent teacher organization, kindergarten through third grade."

A sharp look from Emily shut them up. "If Saturday is the *only* day you saw Jenny, line up here." She taped a page labeled Saturday to the wall. "Sundays only, here. Mondays there. If you saw her multiple times, go to the most recent day. Talk among yourselves, *quietly*, and write down who she talked to, what she had with her, how she acted, if you saw her somewhere other than here, and for Monday folks, what was she wearing, did you see her leave."

"Hey, you two, get that roll of packing paper from the storage room. And a box of Sharpies." Bobby's assistants pushed tables together and rolled out the paper. "We're gonna make a timeline. Where you saw her, when, what she was doing."

Saturday, Jenny'd been at Bobby's twice. Someone saw her at Whole Foods, putting a Good Times flyer on the bulletin board. Times and notations of who else might have been around were scribbled as the Sunday people chatted. Sunday sightings were soon filled up.

"Um, Bobby? I saw Jenny on Sunday. Her flyer caught my attention and we talked. She showed me a photo of a calico cat, up for adoption at the Good Times shelter. I put my application in." Bethie took a deep breath. "The shelter just texted me to ask why I haven't been by to pick up the cat. They told Jenny on Monday I was approved and she was excited to tell me herself. They haven't heard from her. If I'd just checked…" Bethie was near tears.

"She was here Monday. I wanted to talk to her but by the time I got my drink, she was gone," Complicated Drink Guy said. "Didn't see her leave."

Josh stood in the open doorway. "What's going on? It looks like speed dating. Why wasn't I invited? No? What's wrong?"

Bobby B brought him up to speed.

"Yeah, I saw her. Monday, I think it was. Yeah, I said Wednesday would be corn chowder day and I'd save her a bowl or two plus cheddar biscuits. She never misses chowder and biscuits day, but she was a no-show yesterday, first time ever."

"Hey, that's right. We made plans for drinks tomorrow night. My crummy boss decided I have to work late," Sue Ann said. "I left a message for Jenny on Monday evening but never heard back. I totally forgot."

"She wasn't here that long on Monday. I started to get her eclair and she came this way but talked to you, Bobby. You took her laptop and put it under the counter."

"Damn, that was Monday?" Bobby scrounged under the counter. "Who put this bale of napkins out here? They belong in the storeroom. Here it is. She's never without this thing. You all keep talking and mapping out what you remember. I'm calling Pete."

*****

The door was locked and didn't budge when I tried to crash it like they do in the movies. Didn't do my shoulder any good. The window was nailed shut, nothing around that resembled a tool anyway, no one walking below, at least that I could see. A good view of a vacant building across the street. Just guessing, I was at least four floors up, high enough a jump would flatten me like I'd been steamrollered. Guaranteed, I wouldn't pop back up like Wile E. Coyote.

There was a TV tray stacked with bottles of room temperature water, sweetened tea, and a bag of snacks. Thank goodness the bathroom worked. Someone must have liked to read in the tub. I found water-damaged romance paperbacks, a few mysteries, and tabloid papers from years ago. At least I'd be entertained. I tested the lights. The bulb in the bathroom was a goner but the one nearest the bed looked new.

I gave some thought to screaming but there were no sounds from outside the door or whatever was next door. The building had the sad feeling of abandonment, much like me. I let out one screech, just in case, got no response, not even an echo. It just made my headache worse. No reason to strain my vocal cords or run into walls until I knew more about what the hell was happening. It would be best to dive into a book and pretend I was somewhere, anywhere, else.

I picked one at random. Really, could fiction be more mysterious than my current predicament? How and when did I get here, where was here, why, and who's behind this? With no answers forthcoming, I settled onto the one chair and started to read about a dead body found in a cupcake bakery. It made me miss Bobby B's. Would they miss me?

*****

Pete arrived at Bobby B's, red lights flashing. "Jenny's missing? What do you know?"

PTO Emily spoke up. "Do you mind?" At Bobby's nod to go ahead, she introduced herself and explained the information gathered so far. Bobby pointed to the timeline.

"I've dispatched a car to her house for a wellness check. They won't break in, but they'll take a close look and question the neighbors. Anybody have an extra key?"

"No key but I know where the spare is." Vanessa spoke up from the kiddie pen. "I delivered a soup and sandwich once when she was on deadline. Look on the third post on the left, under the metal topper thing, she told me in case I got there before she did."

Pete radioed the patrol officers. "While we wait for them to report, let's go over the timeline. If you think of anything else as we talk, call out."

Fifteen minutes later, only a few details had been added when the officers radioed in an 'all clear.' "At least we know she's not sick or hurt at home. Keep working. I'll let the news media know."

"I can help with that. I'm a reporter for the Star." Complicated Drink guy had been two-fingered typing on his mini laptop. "Anybody got a photo of Jenny? My editor's ready to go with the story if you'll give him the okay, Pete."

Things were moving along. No one voiced what was on their minds. Would Jenny be found in time?

*****

When I woke, the headache was worse. I might have thought dehydration but I'd had two bottles of water. It could be hunger. Cheese puffs are fun but not filling. About halfway through the cupcake book, I decided orange fingerprints weren't going to make the book look any worse than it already did so I snacked my way through a medium-sized bag of puffs. I reached for the plastic bag, anticipating pretzels.

I pulled out—a bag of cheese puffs? They weren't there before I slept. I'd eaten those. It took a few minutes, but it came to me. I'd slept for who knows how long when I got here, woke up, wandered around to check out my options, and found I had none for the time being. Then I read, ate, and drank. Slept again. There must be something in the water. I decided to test the tea, drank about a fourth of the bottle. Sure enough, I started to yawn and think about a nap. I did jumping jacks and sang rock and roll songs at top volume, butchering the words, just to keep myself awake.

Judging by the sun or decreasing lack of it, the water had knocked me out for several hours. I still couldn't see anyone on the sidewalk when the few unbroken streetlamps turned on.

When the snack supplier came by next time, I'd be ready.

****

"Oh my, what's all this? Are we playing charades? Emma, look, art projects!" Adelle smiled as Emma steered her toward a vacant table.

"No, ma'am, our friend Jenny has gone missing and we're trying to map out when we saw her last and what might have happened to her," Bobby B explained.

"That lovely girl who talks about dogs and cats? That's a terrible thing," Adelle shook her head. "And to think, I saw her just the other day, didn't I tell you, Emma? Leaving with that man."

Pete was at her table in an instant. "What day? What man? Did you see where they went?"

"Who is this, Bobby?"

"This is Pete. He's the Chief of Detectives, Miz Adelle."

"Oh my, your momma must be so proud." Adelle smiled and patted Pete's hand. "Let's see, I don't remember which day it was but the special was grilled cheese and tomato soup. Like a little picnic, it was."

Bobby said, "That would be Monday. We ran out of soup about three o'clock, so before then."

"Yes, that's right, dear. I believe I got the last bowl. Emma had the side salad instead."

"Who was the man, Miz Adelle?" Bobby sat in the chair across from the women.

"I don't know his name. I just didn't much like his looks, didn't I say so, Emma? They went between the shops here, to his car. Then he got in and drove away."

"What kind of car, color, any detail? You didn't see her walk away?" Pete scribbled notes as fast as he spoke. "The man, he's a stranger to you?"

"Well, it was a dark color, doors in the back, the kind a produce man would drive. Bobby, you know him. Emma and I saw him here over the weekend, must have been Saturday after sewing circle at church. Jenny spoke to him then." Adelle looked up to see Josh nearby. "Josh, he came to see you."

"Me? I have no idea who you're talking about." Josh approached the table. "Are you sure?"

"Yes, he brought you a package. He spoke English quite well for a Frenchman."

"Oh, holy crap, Miz Adelle, do you mean the man who brought the French roast? We were just about out when he got here." Josh grabbed a chair and sat.

"I think you're right. I don't really eavesdrop, you know. I just happen to hear things." Adelle smiled. "Could I get a cup of coffee with a lot of cream, please? And a cookie?"

Bobby stood, leaned over, and kissed her on the forehead. "You can have any damn thing you want, Miz Adelle. I think you just gave us the biggest clue we have."

*****

I decided the best time of the day for the snack supplier to be sure I was sleeping was mid-afternoon. At night, he'd have to use a flashlight and that might draw attention. Mornings, I'd be awake. By noon, I'd eat more cheese puffs or pretzels and drink the water or tea which would put me out again for a couple of hours. I'd likely think it was due to boredom.

The bed was a three-quarter size, roomy for a twin, cramped for a full, the sheets halfway between clean and dirty, the pillow worthless for neck support or hugging comfort. I managed to scoot the bed in front of the locked door. It wouldn't stop anyone but it would give me a warning so I could hide behind the bathroom door. Without a weapon, it was the best I could do.

Since my watch, phone, and purse were gone, I guessed the time by the sun, thankful it wasn't a cloudy day. Backtracking time, my last memory was of Monday, I think. From how skanky I felt and probably smelled, I'd been without deodorant for a couple of days, making this Wednesday. Maybe. Oh, my editor was going to be mad about my missing article!

It wasn't but an hour or so later that the door lock clicked. The bed scraped on the buckled floor. I darted into the bathroom, ready for whatever came next.

There were mumbles, just audible over the wood-on-tile noise. I held my breath until I saw a glimpse of fabric between the door and its jamb, then I pushed as hard as I could and let out a banshee cry.

"What the hell, Jenny? I think you broke my nose!"

"You? Are you here to save me or are you the one who put me here?"

"Well, both. Come, sit down." He pulled napkins from a new food bag, something hot inside based on the aromas. My stomach voted eat first, details later but was overruled by my brain, starved as it was.

"I'm not sitting, I'm getting out of here." I started for the door but

83

was pulled back and plopped on the bed. It happened so easily, I knew I wouldn't be able to make my escape with any kind of success.

"This is for your own good. I'm just trying to save you from yourself." He sat next to me, took my hand. "I've tried to call you but always lose my nerve. After we spoke the other day, I knew we have a real connection. We like the same movies. You said you'd been watching me too, like how you know I deliver to the other coffee shops. And we're both self-employed."

"I have to go home. I want to go home, *now!*"

"We'll go somewhere, soon, make our own home. I promise we'll always be together." He stood. "No more Good Time Jenny." He was out the door, locked it again before I could begin to understand what the hell he was talking about. Good Time Jenny? A connection? I didn't even know his name. I knew one thing for sure. I wasn't going to spend my life hiding from a nut job, always looking over my shoulder, unable to write under my own name. One way or another, this was going to end. I'd bet my life on it.

*****

"Listen up! Pete just called. He's found a connection and thinks they might know where Jenny is. He'll let us know as soon as he can."

*****

He showed up early today, full of plans about how we'd be together always, never listened to what I said to the contrary.

"Jenny, we're going to be so happy. Of course, we'll have to move to get away from here, where people know about your past. I'll be able to get delivery work anywhere so it's not a problem." He paced but always between me and the door. I was weak from hunger and thirst and doubted I could outrun him at this point.

"Why don't we go now? It's a nice day out, let's take a walk." I sat near the window, the farthest away from him I could be. Was that a movement I saw? Just a pigeon on the narrow ledge. Damn.

"I have to collect my last paycheck, then we'll leave, tomorrow." He paced faster. "I know you think men are all alike but really, I'm different. You and I? We're meant to be. Forever. I'll never leave you."

That's what I was afraid of.

*****

"The chopper's two minutes out. I want the front and back entrances covered, two men on the basement door. His cousin said he's done this before, fixated on a woman, sure she's crazy about him. Go along with it if you have to. Just make sure Jenny is safe." Pete paused. "He's heard the sirens, seen the lights, he knows we're here. Sniper on the roof across, if he shows a weapon, take the shot."

*****

Even with the windows closed, I could hear approaching sirens. I caught a glimpse of police cars as they screeched to the curb. "They're coming for me. You'd better get out of here."

"We have to stay together. Come on, I know a way out. My cousin told me about it. He manages these buildings, so he knows." He grabbed my hand and dragged me along, up the stairs. He ran, I resisted, up three flights before my energy gave out. I fell and banged my leg hard on a piece of metal sticking up from the edge of the step. I screamed at the sudden pain, but he didn't seem to hear, just pulled me to my feet and up the stairs, me bleeding all the way.

The next floor was the roof access. "See how close the buildings are to each other? We'll jump to the next roof and then escape from there. They'll never think to look for us that way."

"I can't. I'm afraid of heights and I hurt my leg. I can't make the jump."

"But you have to!"

"You go on without me. I'll explain to them, you were just trying to help."

"Oh, sure, sure, right. I'll call you. Jenny, don't change that number. No matter what, I will always find you so we can be together."

I considered the manic look in his eyes and knew he meant it. He would never stop. "You go ahead and jump. I'll be right here where I can see you land. I promise. I always keep my promises."

And I did.

I sat on the roof, right on the gravel, a few feet back from the edge, weak from lack of food, water, decent sleep, blood loss, and fear.

He moved back about ten feet and said, "I love you, Jenny, you make me so happy." Then he ran.

I timed it perfectly. He was just one step away, moving fast, when I rolled in front of him and threw him off balance.

He windmilled his arms but couldn't recover. Just before he went over the shallow wall, he looked back at me, then dropped and disappeared from sight.

I thought of the Irish prayer for the dead. It seemed appropriate for today.

Come On Eileen
Dexys Midnight Runners

Come On Eileen is a song by Dexys Midnight Runners (credited to Dexys Midnight Runners and the Emerald Express), released in the UK in June 1982 as a single from their second studio album Too-Rye-Ay. It reached #1 in the US and was their second #1 hit in the UK.
It was ranked number eighteen on VH1's *100 Greatest Songs of the 1980s.*

Come on Eileen
Joseph S. Walker

Eileen is there in my earliest memory, seven years old to my five, scrambling up the ladder to the slide, turning to hold out her hand and pull me onto the platform beside her. We stand together at the top, looking at the families gathered in her backyard. Maybe it's the Fourth of July. Fathers cluster around a radio, beers in hand, singing along to a Johnnie Ray song. Mothers watch, laughing so hard they cry, then join in. Children run and play, some starting up the ladder after us.

I tug Eileen's hand, pulling her to the slide. "Come on," I say, and as she turns to me her red hair is ablaze in the sun.

*****

That hair ran through my childhood days like a vein through marble. Eileen was the unquestioned ruler of the kids in our neighborhood, organizing games, orchestrating dares, determining through her favors who was privileged and who was outcast. We worshipped her, feared her, coveted the favor of her gaze. She could wrestle boys her age and older into submission, hit a ball clean over her two-story house, tell stories that kept us enthralled, mock teachers until we were rolling on the ground.

Eileen was the pint-sized queen of Doyle Avenue. Her father, Patrick Flynn, was the king of Little Dublin, a city quarter encompassing docks and warehouses, nightclubs and pawn shops, crumbling apartment buildings occupied by waves of Irish immigrants, and expanding suburbs occupied by their children. Mr. Flynn owned a couple of car dealerships and some gas stations, but everybody knew his real occupation. In that part of the city, every dice game, every pimp, every loan shark, and every smash and grab crew put money in Mr. Flynn's pocket. Most of the men in the neighborhood—most of our fathers—worked for him. Some legitimately. Some less so. My father, Noah Walsh, was one, partnered with a stocky, stoic man I never heard called anything but Kelly. They were enforcers, drivers, hijackers, brawlers. Soldiers.

Mr. Flynn was a widower, Eileen's mother having died giving birth to his only child. He always had women around in his big house, some of them called housekeepers or maids or cooks, some of them called other things by the mothers in the neighborhood, when they talked quietly over kitchen tables. A lot of Mr. Flynn's women tried to tame Eileen. They told her it wasn't ladylike to wear denim overalls everywhere, to fight with boys, to curse and spit. She didn't pay any attention to them. They were never around long.

Little Dublin's kids didn't have to be taught respect for Mr. Flynn. It was the air we breathed. We knew not to talk to cops, or ask too many questions about the things our fathers did. We knew that as far as our teachers and other civilians were concerned, Mr. Flynn was a pillar of the community, generous in supporting charities, the first to offer help when a family was in crisis. We knew which streets were ours and which ones belonged to the Italian gangs always trying to take Mr. Flynn's territory, a block at a time. Before we got to high school, we were veterans of unnumbered skirmishes with the kids from their neighborhood.

The summer I was twelve, a group of Italian teens came across us playing baseball in the park. Taunts turned to shoves, then punches. I was knocked to my hands and knees and one of them brought his booted foot down heavily on my left hand, laughing at the small sharp snaps. I howled and rolled onto my back, just in time to see Eileen swinging her bat into his chest, even as he pulled back his foot to kick me in the head. Willie Mays would have been proud of her form. The kid dropped, clutching himself and keening in agony, and the fight was over. The field was ours again.

When the cast came off a month later, three of my fingers jutted out at odd angles. I would never be able to make a fist with that hand. I told the doctors that I closed it in a car door. I told the cops the same. My father and Mr. Flynn could handle dispensing justice better than they could.

When I thanked Eileen, she laughed and tousled my hair. "Nobody messes with my little buddy," she said. "You'd do the same for me, right?"

I would. I was in love with her, which seemed like the most natural thing in the world. Everybody I knew was in love with Eileen Flynn, one way or another.

*****

Four years later, Mr. Flynn threw a party to send Eileen off to college. Everybody from the neighborhood was there, and a lot more people besides. For the first time in my memory Eileen wore a dress, a scarlet sheath that came to her knees and left her shoulders bare. I couldn't stop staring at those shoulders. She and I hadn't talked as often in recent years, rigid high school hierarchies limiting the contact you could have with someone two classes ahead of you. Her senior year, she dated Ronald Glen, the son of her father's main accountant. After Ronald got drafted, she showed no interest in going with anyone else, and I heard they no longer wrote each other weekly letters.

She circled the room, accepting the congratulations of men Mr. Flynn did business with. Every time she turned away from one, his eyes dropped to her ass. Then he looked around quickly to see where her father was.

I went to the basement, where the kids and teenagers congregated. Somebody had the new Stones album and was playing "Paint it Black" over and over, the bass cranked so high that the floor shook. Couples made out on the couch, peeking over each other's shoulders to see who was watching. In the corner farthest from the stairs, sodas were spiked from hidden bottles of scotch and gin. I took one and let the hysterical clashing noise carry me around the fringes of the room, feeling sour and hating everyone. In a week Eileen would be gone. In a week I'd be back in school, kicking myself every time I looked for her scarlet mane in a crowd.

A soft hand touched my arm. I turned and she was there, inches away, her ivory skin glowing in the dim lights. She said something, but all I could hear was Mick Jagger's angry growl. I shook my head and gestured at my ear. She looked around, took my arm, and pulled me into an empty bathroom.

With the door closed it was just possible to talk. She grinned. "You haven't wished me luck, Liam."

"Good luck," I said. I tried to drink from the cup I was holding. She took it from me, sniffed at it, and tilted her head back to drink. I watched the spray of freckles on her white throat as she swallowed.

"I'm glad you're here." She set the empty cup by the sink. She lifted my left hand and inspected the way the last three fingers bent unnaturally. "Your poor hand. I feel so bad that I didn't stop him quicker."

"It could have been worse," I said. "It feels fine. Doesn't hurt."

"That's good." She kept holding the hand.

"I didn't think I'd ever see you in a dress."

Eileen shrugged, irritated. "My father insisted. He said he was entitled to ask one thing after eighteen years." She looked from my hand to my face. "Tell me you'll be joining me in a couple of years."

I didn't get what she meant at first. "College? I don't have the grades."

"You've got two years to get them," she said. She slipped forward and put her arms around me. I breathed in raggedly and hugged her back. I'd hugged her before, of course. Not like this. I leaned my head into her. My lips rested against her bare shoulder and the living warmth of her skin was in every breath I took.

*****

I walked home right after that. I couldn't face just following her around the party, seeing who else she hugged, seeing who she hugged longer.

There was nobody else I wanted to talk to, and my house was less than a block away. For most of the way I could still hear that damned Stones song.

I was a little buzzed. I went to the kitchen and made myself another drink, a big one, and drank it as quickly as I could, looking at my reflection in the window. I'd only been drunk a couple of times. I didn't really know what the hell I was doing. I felt mean and small and alone and didn't want to feel any other way. I rinsed out the glass and went into the living room and turned on the TV with the volume low. Something to rest my eyes on.

The next thing I was aware of was somebody shaking my shoulder roughly and saying my name. I jerked and rolled to the floor in front of the couch, thinking for a moment I was going to puke. My head throbbed to a long, deep pulse that sent ripples of nausea through me every time it crested.

"Christ everloving." Somebody yanked me from the floor and put me back on the couch. Kelly. He leaned forward and sniffed my breath, grimacing. "You pick tonight for your first bender."

"I'm okay," I managed. "Just need sleep." The only light in the room was from the TV test pattern.

"No time, kid. You gotta come with me. Right now." He yanked me to my feet.

I groaned, dragging my feet as Kelly pulled me to the front door. I tried feebly to pull back, but Kelly was a thick plug of muscle. The state I was in, he could have handled a dozen of me.

Outside, something was off about the peculiar hush of the smallest hours of the morning. I looked up the block. A couple of ambulances and half a dozen police cruisers were parked at crazy angles in front of Mr. Flynn's home. The red and blue rotating lights made the house as garish as a carnival funhouse. Neighbors stood on their lawns in robes. Kelly grabbed my arm and pulled me the other way.

"What's happening?" I asked. "Where are my parents?"

"I'm taking you to your father. Keep quiet. Don't look back."

Kelly's car was parked around the corner. He shoved me into the passenger seat and drove sedately away from the Flynn house, picking up speed only several blocks away.

Nothing seemed real. "I don't understand where we're going."

"Hospital."

I couldn't ask the obvious questions. My breath grew fast and shallow.

Kelly sighed and his shoulders slumped. "I was half your age when my father got it, Liam. It was days before they told me what happened." He drove another half block. "Your mother's dead, son. I'm sorry there's no good way to say that. Your father's in surgery. They were shot."

"The Italians." It seemed obvious. We had wars with Italians, the boogeymen every fretting mother in the neighborhood warned us about.

"No." Kelly licked his lips. "It looks like Mr. Flynn shot them."

He might have been speaking Martian.

"I don't know why," he said. "It was late. Things were winding down. We heard shots upstairs. Me and some of the boys went up and found the three of them in a bedroom. Your folks shot up, Mr. Flynn down on the floor bleeding from a head wound. Before we could even start figuring anything out the cops were there. A woman who didn't know whose house she was in called them, screaming about guns. The boys downstairs didn't know what was going on, but they didn't like a bunch of cops busting in. It got to be kind of a mess."

We were at the hospital. Kelly drove past the emergency entrance and parked in a little lot with a *Doctors Only* sign. We went in a side entrance, past an empty desk, and got into an elevator. Kelly seemed to know where he was going. I didn't try to keep track. The clean-but-ugly hospital smell was killing what was left of my buzz, leaving me with a blinding headache and the sick feeling something was chewing my insides.

On the fifth floor a lot of men, some in uniforms, stood talking in small clusters. Kelly didn't look at them. He took me around a couple of corners, then into a small, deserted waiting room. He steered me into a corner seat, pushing me back easily when I tried to rise.

"Stay in here," he said. "It's important. There's a john behind that door if you need it. Don't stick your head out. Don't go wandering. They'll come tell you when there's something to tell. You got me?"

"Yeah," I said. "My mom's dead?"

Kelly nodded. "I'm sorry, kid. I wish I had something more to give you. You're getting dealt a tough hand, but if I'm in here any longer they'll come drag me out. You're gonna have to play it on your own as best you can." He shook my hand, like it was the only thing he knew to do. Kelly could have thought for a thousand years before it occurred to him to hug me.

I shook off his grip. "*Who* would come drag you?"

He shook his head and walked out.

*****

I was alone for two hours.

I thought a lot about my mother. I'd only recently realized something I should have seen years ago, that she wasn't a happy woman. It's a disturbing thing, understanding your parents are real people with flawed lives that have nothing to do with you.

I thought some about my father. Some about Eileen. I wondered if she saw my parents after it happened. A couple of times I knelt by the toilet, but nothing ever came up. After a while I just stared at the floor. I decided I didn't have to think. There was nothing to think about. I had always been in this room. I always would be.

The man who came in after two hours wore a dark suit. His hair was a tight buzz over rimless glasses. His head was tilted back a little when he came in, and the reflected light turned his eyes into flat featureless white disks. He pulled a chair over and sat directly in front of me, our knees separated by about a foot.

"I'm sorry for your wait, Liam," he said. "There's been a lot happening. I'm Agent Elkhart."

95

Four words had been drilled into me as the only thing I was to ever say to a cop of any kind. "I want a lawyer."

Elkhart's lips thinned. He went on as though I hadn't spoken. "I understand you've been told your mother couldn't be saved. I'm sorry for your loss, son."

"I want a lawyer."

He raised his voice, just a little. "Your father is out of surgery. I've been talking with him. In a few minutes we'll go see him together."

"I want a lawyer."

The flat of Elkhart's hand came down with explosive force on the table beside him, making a noise like a gunshot in the small room. I couldn't keep from jumping. Elkhart's face was strained. "Don't say that again," he said. "I'm trying to go easy because you just lost your mother, but you're not under arrest. I'm not even asking you any questions. You don't need a damned lawyer, especially some mouthpiece from Flynn. All you've got to do is listen."

I crossed my arms to keep from shaking. He rolled his shoulders.

"You didn't get that lawyer stuff from nowhere. You know what your father did for a living and who he did it for. I might as well tell you I've been after your dad for a long time."

And never got him, I thought but didn't say.

"Your father says that he went looking for your mother at the party," Elkhart said. "He found her in an upstairs bedroom with Patrick Flynn. Flynn was ripping her clothes off, trying to force himself on her. You understand what I mean by that, right?"

I didn't speak or move.

"Your father grabbed him and shoved him away. Flynn fell and hit his head hard on a marble table. He thought Flynn was down, so he turned to check on your mother. Then Flynn got a gun from somewhere and started shooting, and he hit them both."

I choked something back. "When can I go home?"

"You can't, Liam. You'll never see that house again." Elkhart leaned forward. "Your father is testifying, son. He's going to give us everything he has on Flynn, the whole operation. He's going into witness protection, and you're going with him."

It was like being kicked in the stomach. "My father's no rat. That's not true."

But it was.

*****

They put us in a little Midwestern house, in a city just big enough that new people in town wouldn't be endlessly discussed. Someone built a ramp to the front door for the chair my father would spend the rest of his life in. The wood wasn't painted or finished, and the ramp still smelled like a lumberyard.

It took a long time to get from the little waiting room to the house. A few hours after his surgery, Elkhart moved my father to a private hospital a hundred miles away. He was there for three months, learning to use the chair, learning the things he could and couldn't do. There were always feds guarding him, and Elkhart came several times and was closed up with him for hours.

My father would barely talk to me. The first time we were alone together I begged him to tell me Elkhart was lying. He rested his head back against his pillow and closed his eyes. "There are things a man doesn't do," he said. "Flynn has it coming."

That was the only thing he ever said to me about the night of Eileen's party.

After the hospital we spent six months in a hotel in Chicago, my father more shrunken and defeated every day. There were always cops around. Several times a week he went to speak to other cops, and lawyers, and, eventually, a grand jury. He barely ate and slept badly, and as the months ground on he grew gaunt and even more silent.

I thought he'd be different once we were on our own, and he was. He was worse. Entire days passed with him simply sitting in the living room, staring at whatever was on TV, not talking. He watched the moon landing and live reports from Vietnam and the Watergate hearings, and never expressed a scrap of interest. The disability payments that were part of his immunity deal paid for nurses to come a few times a day. He never asked me to do a thing for him. He never asked me about school, where I tried to remember to answer to the name Tommy Rogers. He wouldn't speak about my mother or Mr. Flynn. The only person he ever talked to was Elkhart, who came by every month or two to check on us.

I decided both my parents were killed that night at Flynn's. It was just taking my father longer to die.

I graduated high school a year late because of the time I'd lost. Neither of us went to the ceremony. My hand meant that I didn't have to worry about the draft, and as I predicted to Eileen, I didn't have the grades for college. I got a job at a sporting goods store. I went drinking with coworkers at the end of the week, dated a little. But every morning I woke up in the same silent house, smothered by my father's sorrow and rage. I thought about moving out, getting a place of my own, but it felt like leaving things unfinished. My mother would want us together.

Seven years passed that way.

*****

I was twenty-four when I came home from work one day and found my father sitting in the kitchen, obviously waiting for me. He had shoved one of the chairs aside so he could roll up to the table. There was a small leather case in front of him. He told me to sit and rubbed his hands over his face.

"Elkhart was here today," he said. "They let Flynn go."

I frowned. "He was supposed to be inside for life."

"He was. It was the only thing keeping me going. I wanted to still be here when he died. I wanted him to die ugly." His voice sounded rusty.

"What happened?"

His mouth twisted. "Compassionate release," he said, making the words sound filthy. "He has cancer. Supposed to have less than a year."

"Okay," I said. "That sounds like a pretty ugly way to die."

"You're not listening," he said more forcefully. For the first time in years, I heard the man who had taught me to ride a bike, sent me to my

98

room when I misbehaved, sat me down and explained what he did for a living and how the world needed toughness. "The man who killed your mother is free. The man who put me in this damn chair gets to die in a nice comfortable bed with his daughter at his side."

He pushed the case across the table. "Open it."

Inside the case was a clip-on holster, holding a Smith & Wesson revolver with a two-inch barrel. It was the gun my father used when he taught me to shoot, starting the day I turned ten. There was a box of bullets. A zippered vinyl pouch held banded bundles of hundred-dollar bills and a slip of paper with a phone number.

"You're not supposed to have guns," I said. "How did you hide this from Elkhart? Where did the money come from?"

"Elkhart knows what he needs to know," my father said. "Same goes for you."

I put everything back in the case.

"The phone number is Kelly's," he said. "It's only good through the end of the week. Call him when you're close. He should have something for you on where Flynn is."

"Why would Kelly want to help you? Isn't he inside?"

"I gave them squat on Kelly. He only did two years. Anyway, he's never been a man to think about the past. He thinks about the future."

"I'll have to be pretty damn close to use this."

"That's one of the things the money is for. If you see a chance to pick up something better, do it. This is what I can give you right now." He rolled back from the table. "Leave first thing in the morning."

He was starting to turn toward his room when I spoke. "What if I don't want this?"

He didn't look at me. "You're leaving this house tomorrow morning, boy. Now, if you're the kind of lowlife prick who would let his mother's killer walk around free, well, you've got a gun and a few thousand bucks to go start a life somewhere else. Otherwise, you can come back here when it's done."

*****

99

I called Kelly from a gas station phone booth twenty miles from my childhood home. The drive had taken me two days in the used VW Bug I bought a year ago.

"First thing you gotta understand," he said when I told him where I was, "is there's a lot of people in town would shoot your father on sight, and might have the same attitude about you."

"I'll be careful. Where's Flynn?"

"Nobody knows. He went to ground someplace when he got out. There's a feeling he's in the area."

"So I wait?"

"You remember Miriam Pace?"

It was a weird question, but I said sure. "She lived three doors down from us. I think her father sold cars for Mr. Flynn."

"Right. She's getting married Saturday, at the country club."

"That's nice. Where's she registered? I'll pick her out a toaster, maybe."

"Think it through, kid. She and Eileen were pals, right? Flynn won't be there, but I'm betting Eileen will be. And who better to tell you what you need to know?"

*****

The gate across the country club drive was closed. Two guys holding clipboards stood in front of it, bracketing the big PRIVATE EVENT TODAY sign. I drove past, circled around, and parked the VW on a side street where the back yards adjoined the golf course. I remembered stories about older kids parking there late at night so they could go have sex on the eighteenth green.

I'd have to walk in. I wore a windbreaker to cover the gun clipped to my belt and a baseball cap to cover hair exactly the same auburn shade as my father's.

The big parking lot beside the building was full. A driver leaned against a limousine with cans tied to the rear bumper at the main entrance. A few more guys in suits loitered around the entrance. I walked around to the maintenance sheds at the rear and got a rake, then went back and started working on imaginary leaves at the edge of the lot. Nobody paid any attention to me.

Assuming Eileen was in there, she might leave with other people, and without the car I had no way to follow her. I wouldn't be any better off parked out on the road, though, making the guys at the gate curious and just trusting that I'd spot what car she was in. All I could do was trust to luck.

I'd been raking for half an hour when a crowd of well-dressed people came out of the club. The limo driver dropped a cigarette—his third since I'd been watching—and walked around to open the back door. The group milled around, leaving an open path from the club to the limo, and after a couple of minutes Miriam came out in a wedding dress, arm in arm with a guy whose tux was struggling to hold in his gut. They ran for the limo as everyone cheered and showered them with rice.

I barely looked at them. I'd spotted Eileen the moment she came out, that unmistakable flaming hair taking me right back to being a five-year-old at the top of a slide.

I reminded myself to breathe.

The limo pulled away as everyone stood and waved. When it was out of sight, some people headed straight for the parking lot, others breaking into small groups to talk. I leaned the rake against a tree and stood behind a truck, tilting the side mirror so I could watch through the windows. Even in the mirror, Eileen was unmistakable. She talked to some people, hugged a woman, joined a small cluster and seemed to be laughing. She was wearing a red dress and carrying a matching purse.

After fifteen minutes she broke away, giving a couple of final hugs and kissing someone on the cheek. She came into the parking lot, holding her purse up to rummage for keys, and walked right past the rear of the truck I was standing beside. I fell in ten paces behind her. My hands were shoved in the windbreaker's pockets to keep them from shaking.

Eileen found her keys and slung the purse over her shoulder. Thirty yards from the building, she turned sharply right, between two big panel vans with the logos of a florist and a caterer. I was about a second and a half behind her. I turned between the vans. She was nowhere in sight.

I stopped, confused, and an arm came around from behind me and clamped across my windpipe. It was slender, but strong, and the grip was tight.

"You picked the wrong girl to follow, creep," a familiar voice said in my ear. "This how you get your kicks? You a pervert or just a purse snatcher?"

I couldn't get the breath to speak. I put my hands on her arm and tried uselessly to pull it away.

"Don't bother fighting," Eileen said. "You'll be out in a minute."

My head started to swim. I took my left hand off her arm and held it up in front of us, waving it desperately, the three fingers bent back. A shudder went through the body behind me and the arm let go. I stumbled forward, coughing, and just managed to keep my feet.

"Mother of God," she said. "Liam."

"Nice to see you too." I was barely able to wheeze it out.

"What the hell are you doing? There's at least three guys here who'd love nothing more than the chance to beat you bloody."

"I had to see you," I said. I rubbed the front of my throat, listening to my voice come back. "This was all I could think of."

"All you could think of? Did you try the phone book? I'm listed."

"Oh," I said. "I probably would have thought of that at some point."

"Mother of God," she said again. "Bright boy like you going around armed is a danger to the world."

I reflexively put my hand on my holster. It was empty. She held out her hand, the small gun resting on her palm.

I took it. "I don't think I'm the dangerous one."

"We have to get you away. Do you have a car?"

"Not here."

"We'll take mine. Keep the hat on and move fast. You've already been luckier than you deserve."

*****

Eileen's car was a green sedan a couple of years old. We were ten minutes away from the country club before I could think of anything to say. Sitting next to her felt unreal. I kept expecting to wake up. Maybe the same feeling kept her quiet.

"Where we going?" I finally said.

"I have an apartment on Becket."

"There are things we need to talk about."

"Not in the car." Her eyes were shining.

Looking at her for more than a few seconds was painful. I looked out the window instead. I recognized landmarks, but a lot had changed. There was more graffiti than there used to be. More chain link fences around yards, a lot of them sagging. More houses that needed paint and lawns that hadn't been mowed. More empty places with faded For Sale signs out front. The people walking on the streets had sunken, beatdown eyes.

We went down Doyle. The house she grew up in was split up into apartments. The house I grew up in was gone, just a vacant lot.

"What happened here?"

"Your place?" She didn't look at me. "Somebody burned it down after the first time your father testified."

I wondered if my father knew about that. "I mean the whole neighborhood. Things round here have changed."

"My father." She cleared her throat and started again. "My father and most of the people he worked with went away. A lot of people on the legit side of what he did lost their jobs, moved. The Italians took over. They're harder on Irish-owned businesses than they need to be. Then the plants started closing. That wasn't the Italians' fault, but the whole area has gone downhill."

The apartment building on Becket was ten stories tall with an underground garage. Eileen's apartment was on the eighth floor. It was small but neatly furnished, with books and magazines scattered around.

Black and white photos hung on the walls, showing places I recognized from around the city. I looked at them and then stood at the window. The sun was starting to go down, but you could just see the river a few miles away. I had no idea how to begin talking to her.

"I waited for you," Eileen said.

I turned. She stood with her arms crossed. Even in the dim room her hair shone.

"I thought you'd show up at my college. I kept imagining running into you on campus one day. You'd have a different name. Maybe dyed hair."

"I don't think the feds would have let me go near you," I said. "Anyway, I told you I didn't have the grades."

"And I told you that you had time to get them."

"I didn't think you'd want to see a rat's son."

"You're not your father, Liam. And I'm not mine."

I could have asked her then where Mr. Flynn was.

"You obviously graduated. You're doing well."

"Accounting degree," she said. "Lose money or make money, you need somebody to count it."

"Do you work for your father?"

"No. I never have. I never will."

"Well, I sell sporting goods," I said. "Real growth field."

She took a couple of steps closer to me. "Are we going to keep talking like this?"

"Like what?" The building was very quiet. There was the whisper of air conditioning, but no traffic noise, no birds, no breeze through the treetops.

"Like we haven't known each other our whole lives. Like we don't love each other."

She came still closer.

"What would you suggest?" My voice seemed louder than I intended.

She gestured at a doorway. "The bedroom's through there."

*****

Some hours later I was lying behind her, her head pillowed against my right arm, my left hand moving idly in soft patterns against her skin. The room was dark, but a shaft of light from the hallway fell across her red dress pooled on the floor.

"Is that the same dress you were wearing the night of the party?"

"Still fits," she said. "Only dress I've ever owned. No, wait, that's not true. I have a black one for funerals." She rolled to face me and snuggled deeper into my arms. "Do you really want to talk about my clothes right now?"

"I can think of better options," I said.

*****

When I woke in the morning, she was sitting at a dressing table in the corner, wearing a bathrobe and running a brush through her hair. She saw me in the mirror as I propped myself up on an elbow to watch her.

"One hundred strokes every morning," she said. "Only girly thing about me."

"I beg to differ."

She smiled, but there was something sad about it. She put down the brush and turned to face me. "I've wanted this to happen for ten years," she said. "And now it has, but that's not why you came back. Is it?"

"Let's pretend it is."

"Pretend time is over, Liam. Ask me what you need to ask me."

I sat up. "All right. Where's your father?"

She was quiet for a long moment before she spoke. "He's at a farmhouse half an hour outside town. He has two men with him. One always sits in a little booth with a shotgun, guarding the road up to the house. He says when the time is right, he'll come take it all over again."

"Is there anything left to take over?"

"Not much. But it's what he is."

"Will you take me to him?"

"You and your gun?"

"Me and my gun."

"Yes, Liam. I'll take you to him."

*****

Ten minutes from the farmhouse, Eileen pulled over and I got into the trunk. She was wearing denim overalls over a t-shirt now, the kind of outfit she always wore as a kid, the kind of outfit she was wearing when she broke the ribs of a kid trying to cripple me. She kissed me before she closed me into the dark, cramped space.

After a short, bumpy ride the car stopped again. I heard voices. "Good morning, Jamie."

"Miss Flynn," a deep voice said from outside the car.

"Do you know if he's up?"

"Imagine so. Barry just went into town for groceries, so I'm not sure there's much up there for breakfast."

"I just need to talk to him."

"Okay then." A palm slapped the top of the car. "Have a good one."

"You too."

The next couple of minutes were very bumpy. You don't think about how uncomfortable a trunk is until you have to ride in one. When she let me out, we were near the back door of a rambling old farmhouse that had recently been repainted. We walked through into a long narrow kitchen. The next room was a dining room. Patrick Flynn was sitting at the table with a cup of coffee and a newspaper.

"Daddy," Eileen said. "You have a guest."

The lines on his face were a little deeper, and his black hair was obviously dyed, but Mr. Flynn mostly looked the same as the last time I had seen him, only wearing a sleeveless undershirt instead of a suit. When he saw me, his mouth tightened. He folded the paper and set it to the side.

"Liam Walsh," he said. "Though I imagine you have a different name now."

"Tommy Rogers," I said. "But Liam will do."

He nodded and looked at Eileen. "I suppose I should have expected this. When have you ever done what I wished?"

"More often than I should have," she said. She pulled a chair from

106

the table, set it against the wall, and sat. I took the seat opposite Mr. Flynn and set the revolver on the table in front of me.

He didn't look at it. "How is your father?"

"Crippled. Pissed off. Generally unpleasant to be around. How are you? You don't seem like a man with terminal cancer."

He smiled a little. "Prison doctors are like other men, lad. They need money. They have families they don't wish to see hurt."

"So you're back," I said. "From what I've seen you don't have much to come back to."

"So young," he said. "So clever. Maybe too young and clever. I'm old and crafty, boy, and I've built something from nothing before."

I put my hand on the gun. "Could be you're not going to get the chance."

"Look at that hand tremble. I don't think you're a killer, Liam. You're not your father."

"I don't want to be," I said. "But this is something else. You killed my mother. You tried to rape her."

He blinked. "That's what your father told you?"

"Yes."

He shook his head, seeming genuinely sad. "I've never taken a woman by force, boy. Your mother was a fine woman. Unhappy, but filled with . . . grace, I suppose. Something your father could never see or appreciate. I could."

"So you're saying, what? She came on to you that night?"

He laughed. "That night? We'd been sleeping together for five years. I'll admit we were foolish to try to take a quiet moment together with so many people in the house."

I stared at him. Eileen looked back and forth between us.

"Your father knew, of course. He thought allowing it would help him move up. He had ambitions."

I felt the sick gnawing inside, familiar from the waiting room all those years ago.

"I don't know what changed that night, why he was suddenly angry about it. He burst in and hit me over the head with something, knocked me silly for a minute. I cleared my head just in time to hear the gun. That's when he shot your mother."

The gnawing went away. I just felt cold. I heard Eileen's shuddering breath.

"I got the gun away from him. I suppose you can figure the rest." His eyes dropped to the gun. "I don't think I'm the one you need to be using that on, son."

I picked up the gun and rested my hand on the table, pointing it at him. He stiffened a little. I looked at Eileen. "I don't know which of them to believe," I said.

She shook her head. "I don't either. My father has done some horrible things."

"Mine too." I looked at Mr. Flynn, then back at her. "Would you miss him?"

Her eyes were large. "Yes," she said. "But I'd miss the version of him I believed in when I was eight years old. And the truth is I've been missing that for a long time."

"You were always ungrateful," Mr. Flynn said.

"Shut up," I said without thinking.

It shocked us all a little. The way I was raised, telling Mr. Flynn to shut up was like spitting on a Bible. Beyond conception. But the sky didn't fall in.

"I've been missing my father too," I said. "But I think they're both gone."

"I'm right here, boy," Mr. Flynn said.

I didn't look at him. I looked at his daughter. "If I go away," I said, "and don't come back, not to either of them, not ever. Will you come with me?"

"Yes," she said immediately.

"Wait a minute," Mr. Flynn said.

I stood up and held my twisted hand to her. "Come on, Eileen," I said. She took my hand. Mr. Flynn started to rise, and I pointed the gun directly at his face. He sank back down into the chair.

*****

Jamie looked startled when Eileen drove back down the road with me in the passenger seat. Before he could do anything about it, we were past and heading for the nearest highway.

"Where to?" Eileen asked.

"I think north," I said. "What the hell, let's give Canada a try."

"Sounds good," she said, and she reached over to take my hand. The sky was big and blue and perfect, and I began to hum under my breath, *toora loora toora loo rye ay*, feeling I could sing the song forever.

It's Raining Men
The Weather Girls

It's Raining Men was first distributed to dance club DJs in the US in mid-1982, with the official singles (7 & 12 inch) following on September 10, 1982. Shortly after the release of the single, the *Two Tons* changed their name to the Weather Girls after much confusion by press and fans due to the duo introducing themselves as "the weather girls" in the introduction of the song.

Although it had not yet been released to retail stores, the single gained much attention based on heavy rotation alone. On the chart dated December 24, 1982, *It's Raining Men* reached #1 on the *Billboard* Dance Chart and held the top position for a total of two weeks.

It's Raining Men!
Wendy Harrison

I have found myself in more than one strange situation since I opened my private investigator agency a year ago. Okay, so agency may be an exaggeration. It's only me, Zoe Tanner, but word had spread. I was at the point where I could pick and choose the cases I worked on, but I have to admit that this one, I didn't see coming.

Ozzie Olsen sat across from me at the antique oak desk paid for with some of my separation pay from the Army. Two tours in Afghanistan as an MP ended when I decked my captain who wouldn't take no for an answer. I avoided a court martial and left with an honorable discharge. A trial would've opened a can of worms the powers that be preferred to avoid. I deserved a treat and the desk was it.

"I have a problem." The paunchy but compact man facing me looked uncomfortable. "But I can't go to the police."

"Don't worry about it. If I think I can help, I'll tell you. If not, I can give you the name of a cop you can talk to." Detective Sandy MacKinnon was someone I trusted completely, even if I did have to mislead him from time to time. We were more than friends and had benefits that could rattle the windows.

"Have you heard of 'It's Raining Men'"? I nodded and started to hum the chorus.

He attempted a smile. I could tell he had heard this before. "Not the song. The club." When I tilted my head, he got the message. "It's a kind of nightclub." Still tilted. "You might have heard it called a strip club." Lightbulb.

"Shouldn't it be called 'It's Raining Women'?"

His smile became more genuine. "It's *for* women. Male strippers."

"Is that why you can't go to the police?"

He explained that his enterprise was perfectly legal. He even had the Better Business Bureau's A rating. Who knew?

"I think someone in the club may be dealing drugs. I can't have that. If I ask the police to look into it, they'll scare off the customers, not to mention my best dancers. If you can find out who's involved, I can get rid of them."

He stopped when he noticed my frown. "By firing. No rough stuff. Can you help me?"

We discussed my hourly fee plus expenses, and he wrote me a satisfactory check as an advance. I didn't take credit cards or PayPal. Cash or check only, but I wouldn't start work until I made sure the check was good.

"Do you want me to go undercover as an employee? I can wait tables in a pinch or even tend bar."

"It might be easier if you come in as a customer. We have regulars, so no one would wonder why you were coming back so often."

I chewed on that. Were there some women who were regulars at male strip clubs? I had no idea, but I have to admit, I was looking forward to this assignment.

After cashing the check the next day, I spent some time deciding what to wear to a strip club. I wanted to blend in but had no idea what a woman would wear to ogle nearly naked men. With my carefully honed investigative skills, I turned to Google and was surprised to discover these clubs were in every large city in Florida, and a lot of smaller ones, like ours. From what I could see in the promotional photos, the audiences contained women of all ages. I swore I could see a couple of canes and even a walker parked at the table of more than one of them. "You go, girl," I told the computer monitor images. Clothing ranged from jeans and glittery shirts to revealing party dresses. Judging by the number of photos with at least one partier with a bridal veil draped around a drunken grin, I concluded this was a popular way to celebrate an upcoming wedding.

I settled on black pants and a gray tunic top which hinted at the cleavage within. I could hide the gun at my waist under the loose shirt, not that I expected to need it. The audience was there to have a good time. What could possibly go wrong?

I arrived at the club in time for the evening performance. It was a Friday night. The place was crowded and rang with the noise of laughter and recorded rock and roll. Ozzie had suggested I find a table with an empty chair and sit there. No one would question the addition of an unfamiliar face, especially if I arrived after the women had time to get at least a little drunk. The best candidate for a seat was at a large table right in front of the stage. I was going to get up close and personal with the performers. Even if I didn't find any drug dealing, at least it wasn't going to be boring. I reminded myself to be sure to stuff some bills in a performer's g-string when the dancing started. Just so I'd fit in, of course.

My table was one of those bridal stag parties I noticed online. The bride-to-be wore the requisite white lace on her head. I could tell the two older women across from her, looking uncomfortable, were the mothers of the bride and groom. Judging by the number of glasses on the table, the rest of the group were going to be miserable the next morning when the party aftereffects caught up with them.

Ozzie's voice came over the sound system as the music was cut off. He announced that the "boys" would be on in 15 minutes and to be sure to order drinks and food now. I decided to head for the bathroom while I had the chance.

As I sat in a stall, pondering how I was going to find the phantom drug dealer, I heard voices coming from near the sink. I couldn't believe my luck. Nothing is that easy. But for once, this one was.

"How much for three?" The voice was young and tentative.

"Three what?" Not quite as young, and certainly not tentative. "E? Oxy? Addies?" The New York accent was unmistakeable.

"E?" She still didn't sound sure.

"Seventy-five."

Silence. Then, "Dollars?"

Laughter. "Yeah, dollars. What'd ya think? Bitcoin?"

I waited to see if the customer would be scared off. Unfortunately, not.

As much as I wanted to get a look at the seller, I decided it was too early to blow my cover. As soon as I heard them leave, I followed them out.

The lights dimmed as I reached the table, and applause began as an old Bruce Springsteen song blasted over the sound system. Six men danced onto the stage, wearing denim shorts and tool belts slung low, showcasing their attributes, with their shirts unbuttoned to show off well-oiled chests. The women around me screamed their approval as the men moved in unsubtle ways to the sound of "Working on the Highway." I admired their choreography and then had a lot more to admire as they began to shed items of clothing. As they tore off their shirts, I hoped Velcro was involved. No one would want to have to resew all those buttons after every performance. When the pants followed the shirts, the men left the stage, one by one, to continue dancing between the tables.

I watched as they writhed in front of women who rewarded their efforts with money stuffed into their g-strings. I had brought some singles with me, but as the men moved around, I could see denominations of as much as one-hundred-dollar bills. I hoped I wouldn't be picked for attention. A couple of singles didn't seem like a good idea.

Just then, as I looked up, one of the men danced towards me. I was relieved when he kept moving until I realized I knew him. I hadn't seen him in years, but there was no mistaking the freckle-faced redhead who used to tag after Catie and me. She was his older sister and my best friend. One day, when we chased him away as we often did, he tripped and fell into a cement sluice diverting water down a hill in the park where we played. He broke his arm and was left with a scar running from the edge of his left eye down his cheek in a zigzag shape I would never forget. It was pale now, but unmistakeable. Adam Wilkins. A male stripper. What would Catie say? We'd lost touch when I went to Afghanistan. I wondered if she knew what he was up to.

When he passed to get back to the stage, he looked at me and jerked to a stop.

"Hi, Adam," I said, making sure to keep my eyes focused on his face and nothing lower.

"Zoe?" When I nodded, he grinned and said, "I thought you went off to war."

"I did. But I'm home now."

He looked around. "I have to get changed for the next number. Don't leave before we can talk. Catie will never believe this."

Seeing him brought back memories of a childhood that felt safe and a time when I was free of the rage that ignited in me now with the smallest trigger. Coming back to my hometown was looking like a good decision.

When the intermission started, I walked around, listening for the voice of the woman in the bathroom. I was sure I'd know it when I heard it, but the noise level of happy, drunk, aroused women didn't lend itself to eavesdropping. As I passed the bar on the side of the room, I stopped to order a tonic and lime. I was working and needed a clear head. It wasn't easy to get the bartender's attention while she was shouted at by a mob of customers and servers. When she finally turned to me, I told her what I wanted and added, "They should get you some help, Alice." It wasn't a lucky guess. The name tag on her shirt was a clue.

"No kidding." She looked around. "Roz was here a minute ago. What was she thinking, taking a break when the dancers did. That's when we're always slammed." She put my drink in front of me, and I put enough money down to include a fat tip. I'd had jobs like this, underappreciated and underpaid. I hoped to talk to her when things slowed down to see if she knew anything about drugs in the club. It wouldn't hurt to have her remember me kindly.

Intermission was over by the time I finished my drink and returned to my seat. The whooping and hollering began again as the dancers strutted out to the sound of "It's Raining Men." I didn't think the place could get any louder, but I was wrong. The titular song of the club turned the women into shrieking valkyries. I wished I had the sore throat lozenge concession.

As the men twirled large red umbrellas, I realized someone was missing. There were five of them, and no sign of Adam. I stood and sidled through the small aisle between the table and the front of the stage. A door led to the backstage area. It was a relief to close it behind me and cut the noise to a loud hum. I walked along a passageway and reached a large open dressing area. There were mirrors along the walls with small tables in front of them with scattered makeup, spray tan, combs and the rest of the requirements of the job.

"Adam?" I called his name but it was clear it was empty. Another door was at the back of the space. "Adam?" As I knocked, the door opened into a bathroom. Sprawled on the tile floor was Catie's little brother, the metal spike tip of a big red umbrella buried in his bare chest.

I didn't need a medical degree to see he was dead, but I knelt to check for a pulse anyway. He wore a short slick raincoat, open to the waist, like the dancers in the It's Raining Men song. The pesky kid brother was gone, and I hoped I wasn't going to have to be the one to tell Catie. Rage grew in the pit of my stomach. As I stood, I forced myself to practice the breathing technique the shrink had taught me. Facing away from Adam's body, I closed my eyes and counted to five as I breathed deeply and then five again as I breathed out. The fire subsided, but enough remained to fuel my need to find whoever killed him.

I reached into my pants pocket and pulled out my phone. Sandy was number one on my speed dial.

"What's up?"

"I'm at 'It's Raining Men.' There's been a murder." There was a moment of silence as he processed what I had said. "It's a strip club," I added, trying to be helpful.

"I know what it is. Who's dead?"

"His name is Adam Wilkins. He's one of the dancers. His body is in the dressing room bathroom. I'm there now, and I'll make sure no one comes in. You're going to have a mob to deal with. The place is jammed."

"Don't touch anything." He hung up before I could tell him where to go. He knew very well this wasn't my first rodeo.

I opened the doors to each of the two stalls with my foot. They swung easily, and I could see no one hiding in them. I backed up until I was in the doorway, then walked back into the dressing area. Some of the mirrors had photos tucked in their frames. I found Adam's space by the picture of him and Catie taken when he graduated high school. I was the one who took it.

Moving as quickly as I could, with the bottom of my shirt covering my hand, I pulled open the drawer under Adam's mirror. Nothing of interest except a key that looked like the kind used in high school lockers. I was tempted, but I knew Sandy would kill me if I took anything from the scene.

It was a good choice because Sandy's voice came from the doorway. "Where is he?"

I could hardly hear him over the noise from the club. "What's going on out there?"

At the sound of my raised voice, Sandy took the hint and closed the door, but his look of disgust answered the question. "Those crazy broads think my guys are part of the act."

"Maybe they'll make a few extra bucks." I started to laugh but stopped when I remembered why he was here. "Adam is in the bathroom down there." I pointed.

Sandy went to check. When he came back, he asked, "How do you know this guy?"

I explained and added, "I was here on a job. It was a crazy coincidence." Our eyes met. "I know. I know. You don't believe in coincidence. I don't either, usually. But it's true this time. And no, I can't tell you who my client is or why I'm here."

We'd been through this before when our professional paths crossed. I had the protection of confidentiality, and Sandy hated it. I hoped the drug dealing I was looking into had nothing to do with Adam's death or I'd be caught between a rock and a hard place, Sandy being the rock and my duty to my client being the rest of it.

Sandy told me to wait in the club to have my statement taken. As I walked down the corridor, a woman rushed toward me. "Where is he? Where's Adam?"

I knew that voice. I grabbed her as she tried to get to the dressing room. "You can't go in there." She was in her 20s, curvy, pretty under heavy makeup. Her clothes were too tight and left nothing to the imagination. Just what I would expect in a girlfriend of the Adam I remembered from his teens.

"Is he all right?" She was crying now. "Please tell me he's okay."

I held onto her and turned her back the way she came. "Come with me. Is there a quiet place we can talk?"

I felt her start to go limp and kept my arm around her. Returning to the mayhem didn't appeal to me. As we passed a door I hadn't noticed earlier, I stopped. "What's in here?"

"It's a break room. For the staff."

I opened the door and pulled her in with me. The small space had a coffee machine and a vending machine with snacks. I sat her at one of the tables and used my dollar bills to get two cups of coffee. I took mine black but loaded hers with cream and sugar.

"I'm Zoe," I said. "Zoe Tanner. What's your name?"

She took a sip of the hot brew. "I'm Lucia Downs. I'm Ozzie's assistant, and Adam is my fiancé. But he's dead, isn't he? All those cops. When he didn't come out for the last number, I knew somethin' awful had happened."

"Why did you think that?" I knew what I was going to hear. "Does it have something to do with the drugs?"

She started to shake her head, but I could see she didn't have the strength to lie. "How'd you know? You a cop?"

I told her I was a private investigator and I had heard her in the bathroom earlier.

"I did it for Adam. We needed the money so we could get married. But never the hard stuff. Only pills. If we didn't do it, someone else would've."

How many times had I heard that excuse? But I needed to move on before Sandy could interrupt us as they searched the club. "Why did you think something bad happened to him?"

She shrugged. "We knew what we were doin' could get us in trouble. But we were gonna stop. Adam had an offer from a casino in Las Vegas. To join their show. It would mean more money. We wouldn't need to do, you know, anymore." She looked at me with teary eyes. "You should talk to Johnny."

"Who's he?"

"Johnny Grier, one of the dancers. He wanted the Las Vegas gig. He's been all over Adam about it. They had a big blowup last week."

Johnny would be my next stop, but I had a last question for Lucia. "I saw a key in Adam's drawer in the dressing room. Are there lockers here for the dancers?"

She nodded. "In the storeroom. Go past the bar and down the other side of the stage." I guess we hit it off because she lowered her voice and volunteered, "It's where Adam kept the stuff."

Now I had to figure out how to get into the locker before Sandy could follow up on the key he would certainly find where I left it. I regretted not taking it. No good deed….

I left her to cry it out and went back out into the chaos. The police had done a good job of quieting things down. The dancers all sat at the front table, and the customers had been herded into the ones behind them. Considering the state of undress of the men, I hoped for their sake the chairs were more comfortable than they looked.

As the police took a statement from each of the ladies whose fun night out had turned either disastrous or more interesting, depending on their bent, they sent them on their way. Most of them would be able to alibi the others at their table. The time of death was no mystery. Between the end of "Working on the Highway" and the start of "It's Raining Men" narrowed it down considerably. If someone other than one of the dancers killed Adam, how would they have done it without being seen? And how could the others not have noticed Adam didn't come out of the dressing room with them? Did this have anything to do with drugs or was there another reason to kill poor Adam?

I thought again about Catie. I was sure Sandy wouldn't want me to be the one to tell her. They had a procedure for death notifications, but as soon as I could, I'd go see her. I hoped I'd have some answers for her by then.

When I realized the cops would be questioning the dancers last, I walked over to the table. The five men looked at me as I took an empty chair.

"Terrible thing," I said.

"Adam's dead, isn't he?" The blond's lips quivered. For the first time, I noticed the hair of each of the men was a different color. Brown, black, blond, silver, none-at-all. Adam had filled the redhead slot. Something for everyone.

None-at-all spoke up. "We're not idiots. All these cops? And Adam not here? Don't have to be Sherlock Holmes to guess something happened to him."

I figured I wasn't sharing state secrets. "Yes. Adam's dead. When did you all see him last?"

Brown answered with a question of his own. "You a cop?"

I shook my head. "No." It wasn't a lie. I thought they might be more likely to talk to me if they thought I had a personal interest in what happened. "Adam's sister is my best friend. I've known him since he was a kid. So, when did you see him last?"

"We were all in the dressing room after the highway number. Adam always went to the bathroom at the end of our breaks. We kidded him about it, but he'd just laugh." There were nods around the table. I wondered if Adam was taking some of his own product to get through the high-energy performances.

"He always came out last onto the stage. We didn't think anything of it until we started the number and saw he wasn't there."

"Which of you came out last instead?" They all looked at Silver. Despite his hair color, he didn't look any older than the rest of them. Maybe it was a marketing tool for the older women.

When Silver stayed quiet, I asked, "And you are?"

He glared at me. "Johnny Grier. And I didn't do nothin'."

"How far behind the others were you?"

He considered the question. I could tell he was calculating how much he could bend the truth without the others jumping in. "I had some trouble with my umbrella. It was sticking when I tried to open it. It took a minute to get it to work before I went out on the stage."

I saw a few surprised looks and one raised eyebrow. Something to follow up later. Right now, I spotted Sandy heading toward us. I jumped up and was halfway across the room by the time he arrived at the table. I felt him give me the stink eye, but I kept moving.

A second bartender was standing behind the bar. Alice was next to her, and both of them looked dazed. The cops must've told them about Adam. I walked over to them. "How're you doing?"

Alice shook her head. "I can't believe it. Adam was one of the good ones. Funny. Polite. Never hit on me."

"You must be Roz," I said to the other woman. She looked startled.

"Do I know you?"

"Alice mentioned your name before." I didn't state the obvious. Her nametag was a dead giveaway. Roz was older than Alice but in good shape for what I guessed to be around 40. She must have had mad bartending skills to be hired in a place where no one except Ozzie seemed to be over 30. She wore the same "It's Raining Men" t-shirt as Alice, but she didn't fill it out quite as much. I noticed a gold locket that hung down above the "Raining."

"It's beautiful," I said, and leaned forward to get a closer look. "The etching is exquisite."

She held it out so I could see it more easily. "Does it open?"

She hesitated and then pulled the small cover open. Inside was a picture of a teenage girl with a sweet smile.

"Your daughter?" She nodded. "She's lovely."

"Thank you. She was."

Before I could ask any more questions, I could hear Sandy's voice across the room. Hoping he didn't see me, I continued on my way to the locker room behind the right side of the stage. I made it without interruption and entered a room with a line of lockers on one wall. There were a dozen or so. Six dancers, two bartenders and a handful of servers. I guessed Ozzie figured that was all he needed to supply. Sandy would no doubt have the key as soon as the cops searched the dressing room so time was short. I couldn't see myself breaking into all the lockers, looking for Adam's, but with my sharp detecting skills, I deduced that the names written on the lockers solved my problem.

I picked the lock easily, one of my many semi-illegal skills. Inside, I found Adam's street clothes with his wallet and car keys. It made sense. There was no place to carry any of it when he was in his work outfits. There was also a duffle bag, and I hesitated before I pulled the zipper open. I knew what I'd find, and it broke my heart. Baggies of pills, carefully labeled. Wouldn't want to sell someone Adderall when they wanted Ecstasy.

I closed the duffle and left it in place. Adam's wallet was next. I found it stuffed with cash, but I was more interested in the plastic wallet insert. It held a smaller copy of the photo from his dressing table mirror, the picture of him and Catie. There was another photo in the insert, facing out behind the first one. It was a glamor shot of Lucia. As I started to close the wallet, I realized there was something stuck between the two photos. I eased it out. It was the same picture as the one in Roz's locket, the one of the daughter who *was* lovely.

I returned everything to the locker and closed it, leaving it unlocked. This time, I wasn't filled with rage, just regret for how this was going to turn out.

I found Sandy still at the table with the dancers and walked over to him. "We need to talk."

He stood, told the men to wait for him, and I led him to the locker room. When I showed him what I had found and what I thought it meant, I waited for him to tell me for the hundredth time that I needed to leave the crime solving to the police. Instead, he looked as sad as I felt. He checked inside the locker to confirm what I told him, and we both left the room. He pulled one of the cops aside and told him to make sure no one went into the locker room, and we walked together to the bar.

Roz watched us come toward her. For once, Sandy let me take the lead. I touched her arm. "We know about Adam and your daughter." As she fought back tears, I felt awful but I knew I couldn't stop. "It was the drugs, wasn't it?"

"He killed my baby. Do you have children?" When I shook my head, she said, "I would've done anything to protect her. But I couldn't. She fell for him and wouldn't listen to anything I said. He was too smooth, too charming. Too good to be true. And then he killed her with his drugs."

She stared at me. "When I took the job here, I didn't have a plan. Then I heard everyone joking about how Adam always used the bathroom right before going on stage. That gave me the idea. While they were doing the first number, I took an umbrella from the dressing room and hid in a bathroom stall. I got lucky during the break. No one used the bathroom. But after I heard the dressing room empty out, Adam came in, just like they said he did. At first he thought I was just another female who wanted him, but he stopped laughing when I stabbed him." She turned to Sandy. "He'll never hurt anyone's daughter again."

As Sandy started to cuff her and read her Miranda rights, I turned and left the club to begin the drive to Catie's house. For the first time, I wished I was back in Afghanistan.

Somebody's Watching Me
Rockwell

Somebody's Watching Me" is a song recorded and written by American singer Rockwell, released by Motown in 1984. It was the lead single from his eponymous 1st album, which also featured guest vocals by both Michael and Jermaine Jackson.

Released on January 14th 1984, the song reached #2 in the *Billboard Hot 100*, and #1 in the *Billboard Hot Black Singles*.

Rockwell is a son of Motown CEO Berry Gordy.

Somebody's Watching

Bev Vincent

I watch people for a living. That's probably not what people are thinking when they hire me, but that's the job. These days, most private investigators sit on their asses and do their investigating online, using databases and social media, but that's not me. When you visit the offices of Max Jacobson, Private Investigator, nine times out of ten I'm going to end up following someone.

The best way to find out if someone is being unfaithful is to sit in a car outside their house to see who comes by when no one else is home and tag along after the target anytime they go out. Sit in the parking lot outside their office to see what they get up to during their lunch break. Suspect an employee who filed a workman's comp claim is malingering? The only way to be sure is to follow them to see if they're going to the gym or carrying heavy grocery bags. Some people might call it stalking. To me, it's just part of the job description.

There are, of course, other tricks of the trade. Searching trash cans at the curb is fair game. Eavesdropping on someone on the phone or while they're having a conversation in a semi-public place is another way to gather information. I have no problem spending hours in a car or in the parlor of a house across the street with a pair of high-powered binoculars looking through someone's open living room blinds, even though some people would say that's creepy.

To be honest, there aren't many limits to what I'll do to gather the information I need to satisfy my clients, especially if they're willing to pay for what I call "concierge service." Like I said, searching garbage bins is completely legal. Opening mail, not so much. Following someone from a discreet distance is acceptable behavior. Putting a tracker on a car isn't. Tapping phones, deploying spyware, breaking in to install recording devices, or to hack into computers—any of those activities could land me in jail. That's why my clients pay the big bucks. I provide services most other investigators refuse to do.

You learn a lot by watching a person for days on end. You uncover the things they believe are closely guarded secrets. The illicit rendezvous disguised as business dinners or corporate retreats. Hidden addictions. How lonely many people are, staying up late in the glare of a flickering TV screen or computer monitor, subsisting on frozen dinners and booze.

After a few days of surveillance, I know what kinds of shows people like to watch, who they're in touch with when they're pretending to be doing something else, the things they search for on the internet. A lot of it is mundane. Recipes, movie showtimes, directions, videos about how to repair something. Visits to dating sites, chat rooms. Porn—lots and lots of porn, of an astonishing variety.

Some things I learn, though, are more revealing. One woman neglected to delete her search history after looking for a kind of plant that would make her kids ill without causing permanent harm, part of her strategy to get full custody by accusing her ex-husband of neglect. Of course, the ex-husband couldn't introduce that search history in court because of the way I'd obtained it but, once I knew what to look for, I was able to gather the necessary evidence in a more legitimate manner.

Sometimes I stumble upon evidence of a crime totally unrelated to why I was hired. Generally, I ignore that. It's not up to me to put a stop to every illegal deed being committed in the city. I *did* drop a dime, though, on the guy who killed his girlfriend and stuffed her body in the deep freeze. I was searching his house while he was at work, looking for evidence he was committing corporate espionage. I always check the fridge to get a sense of a person. It struck me as odd that the freezer compartment was stuffed—I mean, packed.

I'd noticed a chest freezer in the garage while obtaining unauthorized access to the house. Imagine my surprise when I popped the lid out of curiosity on my way out. He'd surrounded her body with packages of frozen food and transferred the excess to the refrigerator's freezer. I couldn't turn a blind eye to murder. I have my limits. An anonymous call to the local precinct lit a fire under them and the guy was arrested later the same day. I watched the whole thing, from a safe distance. And my client also got the evidence he needed to prosecute for theft of intellectual property.

I sometimes wonder if the people I'm following sense they're being watched. Characters in books or movies sometimes claim they have a sixth sense about that. They can feel someone's eyes on them, even when the eye in question is a video camera lens, or at the business end of a pair of binoculars or a rifle scope. I can't say that's ever happened to me.

Until last night.

I was lying in bed, the room mostly dark except for the clock radio display and the usual idiot lights on various devices, when I thought I saw a tiny red LED flicker on and off in an unfamiliar location. I tried to ignore it, but it nagged at me. How often had I installed hidden cameras, carefully blocking any giveaway indicators? Why should I think I was immune to someone else doing that to me?

But why would they?

Sure, many people learn one way or another that my work is what got them into trouble. Cost them their jobs, spouses, even their liberty. I'm cautious when I'm out in public because I know some of them hate me for uncovering their secrets. It isn't as if I planted evidence or fabricated testimony, though. I just report the truth, regardless of how I learn it. I always play fair in that regard, no matter how much money a client offers me to lie. I've taken my lumps and given them back in kind. Still, angry people usually come at you in a drunken rage. I couldn't think of a reason why anyone would want to surveil me.

The sensation, though, once implanted, was difficult to shake off. I turned on my bedside light and performed a quick but thorough search for bugs or hidden cameras. I found nothing out of the ordinary. After I turned off the light, I didn't get much sleep. I kept opening my eyes to see if I could catch that flickering LED, even though I was sure I'd imagined it.

Pretty sure, anyway.

Now that I'm up and ready to face the new day, I do a sweep of the entire apartment. Still nothing. I try to push paranoid thoughts from my mind, but it's like deliberately trying to not think about something. Don't picture a purple rhinoceros.

I run anti-malware programs on my laptop and cell phone. Find nothing.

I zone out while taking a shower, trying to organize the day's activities in my mind, but I can't shake the notion that there are eyes on me. It unsettles me. I'm a bashful guy and feel weird that a stranger might be seeing me naked. I worry that if I close my eyes to wash my hair, I'll open them to find someone standing behind me. It's unshakable. Of course, getting soap in my eyes isn't the ideal solution, but that's what happens.

When I open the fridge to get milk for my coffee, I'm certain things have been moved around. The mail on the table by the door is stacked differently. I'm quite sure of it.

The uneasy feeling doesn't go away when I leave my apartment. I pass supposed neighbors in the hallway I've never seen before. The mailman gives me a focused look when I pass him on my way to the parking lot, then goes back to filling mailboxes. He isn't our usual guy, and he looks far too young and buff for the job.

The day feels totally off-kilter. It's nothing to do with my work. I'm following a woman to make sure her workman's comp claim is legit and, by all appearances, it seems to be. Someone is driving her around as she runs errands, and she moves like she's in pain whenever she gets into or out of the car. One stop is at a doctor's office. When I look up the physician, he seems completely above board, not the kind to rubber-stamp a report in return for an under-the-table payoff. Nothing she does leads me to believe she's faking her injury.

The canary yellow Taurus is easy to keep track of. As we travel from place to place, I glance regularly at my rearview mirrors. More than once, I see a black SUV a few cars back, but I can't tell if it's the same one. If I try evasive maneuvers to see if I'm being followed, I'll lose sight of the Taurus. By the time I get home, I have a serious case of the jitters.

I hear strange echoes as I climb the stairs to my second-floor apartment. When I reach the landing, two doors slam shut at the same time. As I walk down the hall, I try to detect shadows behind the viewports to see if people inside the apartments have their eyes pressed against the lenses. I *know* it's crazy. Everyone can't be watching me—can they?

I lock, bolt, and chain my apartment door. The deadbolt feels looser than normal. I disconnect the chain and open the door to inspect the jam, checking for signs of forced entry.

Nothing.

My landline rings. The only people who use that number these days are telemarketers. I pick up, prepared to castigate someone for calling so late, but all I get is dead air. When I hang up, it rings again immediately. More dead air. After this happens a few more times, I unplug the phone from the wall. As soon as I do, my cell phone rings. Unidentified caller. I power it down.

I nuke a frozen dinner and eat in front of the TV. Everything tastes flat. Even the picante sauce lacks its usual punch. The beer is okay, but someone might have doctored it. That would mean they've been in the apartment. I check the door again, this time looking for scratches or other indicators that the lock's been picked. Nothing.

After I stack my dinner dishes in the sink, I turn on my cell phone. Thirteen missed calls, all with no identifiable caller. I turn it off again and leave it in the living room, retreating to the safety of my bedroom. I close the door, something I never do.

I read for a while, but I can't concentrate on the words. Unfamiliar noises keep distracting me, and I constantly scan the darkness for unfamiliar LEDs. Eventually, I turn out the light and try to get to sleep, but the sense that someone is spying on me grows more powerful by the second. If they're watching me, could they still be in the apartment, perhaps hiding in a closet or the shower? Wouldn't I have noticed them when I peed before going to bed? I wonder if there's enough room for them to hide under the bed and fight the urge to check. I can't imagine someone could fit in that small space, but...

I glance at my clock—nearly midnight. The witching hour. The feeling of dread grows stronger until it's palpable. Maybe I'm not being followed by some*one*. Maybe it's some malign force of retribution. I don't believe in evil, but what if evil believes in me?

I'm paralyzed with fear. I can see nothing in the darkness. Or can I? Was that the shadow of someone moving stealthily across the room or was it a figment of my imagination? The little green light on my computer winks out momentarily. Did someone pass in front of it?

I can't take it anymore. I have to get out of here. Reluctant to turn on lights in case of what I might encounter, I fumble in the darkness for my clothes, get dressed and open the bedroom door. I step slowly, quietly into the main room, ears attuned for unusual sounds. It's quiet. Too quiet, but it isn't going to be me who breaks the silence.

I don't need light to navigate. I gather my phone and car keys, then head straight for the door.

I go to remove the chain—it isn't fastened.

I try to disengage the deadbolt—it's already unlocked.

I turn the doorknob, open the door and step into the corridor.

Closing the door behind me, knob turned to minimize sound, I swivel toward the stairs. The hallway lights are turned down low, but emergency lights create pools of illumination. I take one step forward, then another.

The hand that lands on my shoulder is cold, firm, unyielding.

THE DREAM ACADEMY
Produced by Gilmour/Laird-Clowes/
Nicholson

SIDE 1
45 R.P.M.
Time: 4.16
7-28995
MX210379
℗ 1985 WEA
International Inc.

LIFE IN A NORTHERN TOWN

(Laird-Clowes/Gabriel) CBS Songs

Manufactured & Distributed by
WEA Records Pty. Limited

a Warner Communications Company

Life in a Northern Town
The Dream Academy

Life in a Northern Town is the debut single by British band, The Dream Academy, released in March 1985, and it was the lead single from the band's debut studio album. The song originally had a working title of *The Morning Lasted All Day.*

The single reached #7 in the US *Billboard Hot 100* chart in February 1986, and #15 in the UK.

American country music artists Sugarland, Little Big Town, and Jake Owen recorded a live cover version that became a minor U.S. hit in 2008.

Life in a Northern Town

Leone Ciporin

"It's time to leave this town, Brendan. They have good jobs down south and you can stay with me." An off-key trumpet cut off Finn's plea as the high school band rounded the corner, playing *Stars and Stripes Forever.*

A parade wasn't the best time for a heart-to-heart, but Finn had to take what he could get. The town had to take what it could get too, pulling together a Fourth of July parade with an assortment of stragglers, sweeping the town's leftovers into one tidy pile.

The band threaded between Main Street storefronts displaying cheery signs stenciled in windows with painted trim. But most stores were closed or soon would be. Like a fake Western town in a Mel Brooks movie, Main Street was becoming a façade of a town center.

Pebbles crunched under Finn's sneakers as he planted his feet to guard their spot in front of The Crash Pad, a bar whose Sixties vibe once prompted revelers to sing along to the Beatles while swaying under black and white photographs of the Kennedys in the White House. Not anymore. The Crash Pad had crashed for good. No one had even bothered to collect the chairs upended on the tables.

Back then, the town had two grocery stores and a gourmet food shop for those who wanted cheese from exotic cows. Now, the lone grocery store's stock of American cheese risked not making its sell-by date.

The town itself was past its sell-by date, thanks to Grady's decision to move the paper mill, the town's largest employer. People cheered when Grady bought the struggling business years ago from a local family and renamed it after himself. But he'd abandoned that namesake without hesitation, leaving his son, Junior, to finish winding down the business.

Junior was a year ahead of Finn in school, barely noticing him until the day Brendan accidentally brushed Junior's shoulder in the hall. When Junior advanced on Brendan with eager fists, Finn stepped between them, challenging Junior in a voice loud enough to carry to the teacher in the nearest classroom. Finn paid for his defense by becoming Junior's main target for the rest of Junior's senior year. Occasional beatings interspersed with gum smeared on his locker handle, books missing from Finn's desk, or a foot jutting out to trip him. Finn endured it until Junior's graduation granted him a reprieve.

That reprieve ended after Brendan graduated. While Finn's skill with computers had landed him a big city job, Brendan's skills lay with mechanical things, and he took a job at Grady's Mill. Junior would change Brendan's assignments at the last minute, so he'd either arrive too early or miss a shift and be docked pay. Once Brendan started checking his schedule online, Junior pivoted to assigning him the worst shifts. Brendan never reacted, which only made Junior try harder.

Brendan rarely reacted to anything. The only time Finn had ever seen Brendan angry was when Finn took the computer programming job.

"You're abandoning your family." Brendan's normally placid face twitched. "Family is everything."

Brendan had always been loyal. When they played along the river as kids and Finn toppled in, banging his head against a rock, little Brendan pulled him out and washed the wound, his small fingers soothing Finn's stinging skin. When their parents assumed Finn had bruised his cheek saving his brother, Brendan let them believe it.

"I'm not abandoning the family, Brendan," Finn had said as he packed his suitcase. "Just because I'm moving doesn't make me care any less. Family isn't about location."

Brendan had turned his back on Finn and walked away. Though he later hugged Finn goodbye, that hug was more an homage to family than an acceptance of Finn's decision. Finn wasn't sure he'd ever been completely forgiven.

Now, even though Brendan's job at the mill was almost over, neither he nor Ma would move south to join Finn. To them, town and family intertwined.

And Junior hadn't finished with Brendan. While Junior delighted in watching the hope fade from people's eyes as he closed the mill, it wasn't enough to satisfy him. He'd kept Brendan on to wind up the business and serve as a target a while longer.

"Wait it out, Brendan." Sirens pierced the air, and Finn waited until the fire truck passed. "This won't last forever. He'll be gone soon."

"Yesterday, he tripped me and my head hit a paper roller." Brendan rubbed the swelling above his temple, the lump topped by a deep bruise. He whispered, "I'm afraid he'll kill me before he leaves."

Finn swallowed hard. "Move south with me. Today."

"Who'll take care of Ma?" Brendan's pause added the "since you left us."

"Who will take care of Ma if Junior... hurts you?" Finn gripped his brother's arm.

A boy spilled lemonade on Finn's shoes as the Chamber of Commerce float rolled by, with Junior standing under an arch of red, white, and blue bunting. He stared at Finn and closed one eye slowly in a menacing wink before he waved at the crowd, the sun glinting on his watch.

Brendan's arm tensed under Finn's hand. There was only one option left. One way to prove that family was everything for him, too.

The next morning, Finn drove Brendan to work. "I'll bring pizza when I pick you up," Finn told Brendan. "We can have dinner before your next job." With no more excuses for Junior to assign night shifts, Brenda had gotten an evening stint at the auto shop, in the hope that it would become full-time.

That afternoon, after two stops to fill his backpack, Finn drove to Manny's Pizza, tucked along an alley off Main Street. In better days, the alley had featured a sidewalk café, with red and white checkered tablecloths and Italian music. These days, the alley was empty.

"Hey, Manny." Finn greeted him with a half-hug, half-handshake. "Didn't see you at the parade."

Manny's grin revealed a piece of pepperoni between his teeth. "I had a booth in front of the town hall. Sold a lot of pizza."

"Speaking of selling pizza, I need one of your best pepperonis."

"They're all the best." Manny's hands expertly kneaded the dough and topped it with pepperoni. Only one other customer came in while Finn waited.

Once in his car, Finn pulled a canister from his backpack. He sprinkled powder under the pepperonis on one side of the pizza, marking the other side with a pinch of the crust. Then he drove to Grady's Mill.

The brick monolith rose several stories above its neighbors, its height enhanced by the black letters of the Grady's Mill sign scaffolded on the roof. Vertical columns and long windows emphasized the mill's dominance over its surroundings.

With the mill closed, no one greeted Finn as he walked toward the office suite where Junior and Brendan worked. Just before he reached it, he took a sharp left.

The warehouse was nearly empty, with only two rows of paper rolls, and four bales of shredded paper next to the last row. Finn took a bottle from his backpack and ran a thread of gasoline alongside the bales and paper rolls. When he reached the back door, he left a gap, which he sprinkled with wads of recycled paper, to slow the fire's pace.

Finn closed his backpack, grabbed the pizza, and went into the office area. "Brendan?" Finn placed the pizza on the vinyl table. "Ready for dinner?"

"Let me finish this report." Brendan hit a few keys, scraped back his chair, and joined Finn at the table. "Pizza smells good."

"Just picked it up from Manny's." Finn handed Brendan two slices from the clean side of the pie before taking the other two himself, leaving only the powdered half in the box.

Finn waved a slice in the air to spread the aroma. Scent attracted prey and, for once, Junior was the prey, not the predator.

Soon, like a deer aiming for Hosta, Junior ambled into the break room. "Pizza. Just what I needed." He grabbed the pizza box, spun around, and headed back to his office without another word.

Neither Finn nor Brendan said anything either until they finished their pizza. Then Brendan said, "I've got to get to the body shop."

"Sure thing." Finn brushed crumbs from his jeans. "Let me run to the restroom and then we'll be on our way." He trotted down the hall and glanced into Junior's office. Junior's head lay against this chair's headrest, his eyes closed. A small, steady snore confirmed that he was asleep.

Finn walked past the restrooms and entered the warehouse through the back door. He pulled a lighter from his backpack and lit one end of the gasoline thread, a few inches from the first wad of paper.

As soon as it ignited, he sprinted down the hallway, slowing to a walk before he reached Brendan. "I didn't realize how late it was," he told Brendan. "Let's get moving."

Finn glanced in the rearview mirror as they pulled out of the parking lot. A thin wisp of smoke rose behind the letters in the Grady's Mill sign. He'd learn soon enough if his plan had worked.

He had his answer before Brendan got home that night. The flames could be seen all over town, turning the short summer night into dusk. Sirens alerted anyone not looking at the blaze. By the time the sun rose, Grady's Mill had become a giant pile of rubble. The sign that once could be seen miles away was now a stack of charred metal.

One body had been recovered, tentatively identified as Junior. With Junior's unpopularity, and the mill having abandoned the town, there was no outcry for an investigation.

A few days after the fire, Finn steered his grocery cart through the produce aisles, a final errand for his mother before leaving. He nodded at neighbors wearing appropriately mournful faces, occasionally contradicted by a sparkle in their eyes. Finn was careful not to let his own eyes sparkle.

"Brendan still out with friends?" Finn asked Ma as he unloaded the groceries onto her laminate countertop.

"He'll be back soon. Can we drive by the mill before you leave?" Ma spoke in the loudest whisper her lungs allowed. "I want to see it." She propped a crinkled arm on her walker as if to hoist herself out of the massive recliner she'd insisted on keeping after their father died.

"Why do you want to go there, Ma?" Finn stepped into the living room, scraping a stain off a wallpaper flower.

Her eyes narrowed. "I want to see where that… man died." Her lips quivered under her oxygen tube. "I want to spit on his grave."

Finn hadn't considered what Ma had gone through, watching her son's torment and not being able to stop it. Watching his hesitation as he left each morning, and his despair when he returned. Even worse, she knew she was the reason he stayed.

Finn laid a hand on her elbow, her skin shedding like cheap tissue under his palm. "Junior's gone for good, Ma. Put him behind you. He'll never bother Brendan again."

That evening, after Finn and Ma said their goodbyes, Brendan drove him to the train station. It started to rain and Brendan switched on the wipers. "Storm coming," he said.

"If you change your mind, you know you can come south anytime," Finn said. "Family isn't about location."

"I know that, Finn. And I know you'd do anything for family." Brendan flickered a glance at his brother as he pulled into the train station lot. "Anything." The hug he gave his brother was tighter, and longer than when Finn moved away.

Finn joined the sprinkling of passengers on the platform, awaiting the train's approach. He watched Brendan through the drizzle as the train rolled out of the station.

Bitch
Meredith Brooks

Bitch is a song by American singer-songwriter Meredith Brooks and co-written with Shelly Peiken. It was released in March 1997 as the lead single from Brooks' 2nd album, Blurring the Edges.
The song peaked at #2 (for 4 weeks) in the US in the Billboard Hot 100 – and had similar success in Australia, Canada and the UK.

Bitch

Adam Gorgoni

This day doesn't start out differently than any other. Juana rides the 720 bus from Boyle Heights for forty-five minutes, gets off at Wilshire and Rexford, and walks the eight blocks north, uphill to the house. When she reaches the corner, where the front lawn comes into view, she stops to catch her breath and admires the landscaping. Esteban, the gardener, trims the hedges and makes sure flowers are blooming there all year round. He's a good man and meticulous, but he drinks.

Juana has been going to clean the woman's house three times a week for almost eight years now. She takes pride in her work, but the woman almost always finds something to criticize, some overlooked patch of dust on the grand piano (which no one ever plays), or, failing that, she will remind Juana to vacuum under the sofas, or wipe down inside the refrigerator. It's always something.

Because the woman is just a bitch. *Una puta.* Juana doesn't use that kind of language lightly. She doesn't even like to think such things. But there's no other word for this woman, with her puffy lips, her skimpy dresses, and her snotty attitude, a woman who rarely thanks Juana, and who, when she does, says it like she is throwing out a used piece of tissue.

Juana needs the job because it pays better than most. Ever since Mauricio's accident, he hasn't been earning much and Juana is keeping them afloat mostly on her own. She used to drive to work, before the accident, but then they lost the second car and couldn't afford another one on her wages alone. So she takes the bus, walks the hill, three times a week.

And she tries to keep a positive attitude. Because she believes God provides for those who don't complain and try to do the right thing. Yes, lately times have been hard, and she's been having more doubts than usual. But she still believes. After all, they'd made it to California all those years ago and that hadn't been easy. She'd been younger then and pretty. That was why the coyote had picked her out of all the others. She didn't tell Mauricio because she knew that if she did, he would go after the man and the coyotes would kill him. So she bore the indignity and kept going. And God had blessed them. With two beautiful children and a new life far away from El Salvador. They saved for years and were finally able to buy a house of their own. It's a small place— you could fit five or six of them into this house—but it's theirs, and Juana will put up with almost anything to keep it.

She walks through the gate, up the stone path, and pauses again to enjoy the gentle sweetness of Esteban's honeysuckle growing by the front door. Then she breathes deeply and rings the bell. About forty-five seconds pass before she hears the shrill, bleating voice approaching from within.

"Hang on, Carol." The woman opens the door and nods briefly at Juana before turning away and retreating into the den. "I *know!* I just don't understand her. Well, she doesn't know how to handle him anyway."

Juana goes to the small dressing room behind the kitchen, puts her handbag in the closet, ties on her apron, and heads back in. The woman reappears, phone pressed to her ear. "Hold on one more sec, Carol. Juana, I'm having a dinner party tomorrow so make sure to clean the oven today."

Juana tries to swallow her anger. She cleaned the oven last week, and she's willing to bet the woman hasn't used it since.

"Sí, Mrs. Summers," she says to the woman's back because the *puta* is already walking away again. Juana's English is quite good, but in this house, she pretends it isn't. It's just easier that way.

She goes upstairs, strips the beds, puts on the clean sheets, brings all the dirty linens down, and tosses in a load of laundry. She likes to get it going, that way it's in process while she starts her routine. Usually, she will then do all the bathrooms, on both floors. But today, since the woman seems to be camped out on the ground floor, near Mr. Summers' office and the theater—*they have a movie theater in their house, she remembers telling Mauricio*—Juana decides to do the upstairs in its entirety. If she's lucky, she can minimize the instances of contact. When she lugs the mop and bucket up the grand stone staircase she can feel the twinge in her hip that has recently started bothering her. She feels it again when she goes back for the vacuum and drags that up as well. Then she gets started in the kids' rooms.

The Summers children are about the same age as Mari and Jesus, teenagers in high school. When they were younger Juana would pick them up at school and make them snacks while the woman was out playing tennis or shopping or who knew where. But now Charlie, the boy, is off at boarding school and Ashley, the girl, is usually gone before Juana arrives, and doesn't return until after she leaves. The last time she saw Ashley the girl was wearing a top that didn't cover her stomach, and her navel was pierced. The girl had squealed when she saw Juana, and run over for a big, affectionate hug, but then hurried up to her room and closed the door.

Today there is makeup strewn all over Ashley's large, granite-topped vanity. Juana straightens up and wipes down the surface. Next, she disinfects the toilet and mops the floor. When she vacuums under the bed, she finds an empty condom wrapper. She will leave it untouched but it will make her think about Mari. Her daughter has always been smart and sensible. But since she got into that magnet school she's begun staying out later on the weekends, and running with a crowd Juana doesn't know. And she's started wearing more makeup. Mauricio says it's normal at that age and reminds Juana that she did the same. Don't worry, he says. But Juana is not so sure.

She moves on to Charlie's room, which no one uses at present. What kind of people send a thirteen-year-old boy away to boarding school?

When she's finished cleaning, she takes a moment to stare out the window. Out in the yard, past the pool, there is an empty bench under the shade of a sprawling oak tree. A leaf blower drones through the window glass from an adjacent yard.

It's time to do the master bedroom and Juana hopes to get through it quickly in case the woman decides to come upstairs. The bathroom is large, done in elaborate Mexican tiles, with his and hers sinks, lighted mirrors, and a raised Jacuzzi tub. Juana scrubs the tub and toilet bowl (pubic hairs on the rim) and windexes the glass shower doors. As she mops the floor, she remembers the day she dropped a rag and discovered there was heating under the stone that the woman kept going all day long. *Puta.*

A couple of magazines lay face-down near the recliner by the window in the bedroom. *Vanity Fair. Elle.* Occasionally, when the woman isn't home, Juana will stop and page through them. There are a lot more pictures of Latinas these days, but they all look just as fake as the white girls. Today she just arranges the magazines in a neat pile on the end table. By Mr. Summers' bedside, there is a book and a nearly empty water glass.

The woman's dressing table takes up half the wall on the opposite side of the room. Various items are scattered about the surface—perfume bottles, skin creams, costume jewelry, and a tube of toothpaste. Juana begins to gather up the paraphernalia and put it all back where it belongs. Her lips tighten as she removes clumps of brown hair from a round brush. When she opens the top drawer on the right to put the jewelry back in its crystal tray, something odd catches her eye. Lying there in the back corner of the drawer are a pair of earrings that Juana has seen only once or twice—and only in the woman's ears, when the Summerses were all dressed up and going out somewhere fancy. She looks over her shoulder and listens. All is quiet. She reaches into the drawer and feels the weight of the diamonds in her hand. They are heavy. They are real.

What are they doing there? Maybe the woman was drunk late one night and forgot to put them with her good jewelry? Naturally, the woman keeps that stuff hidden away somewhere, as she should; she may be a bitch but she's not stupid, and you can't be too careful. Juana herself keeps her engagement ring and a small wad of emergency cash in a pouch in a shoebox under some old letters at the top of her bedroom closet.

The earrings are stunning. Silver pendants, studded with small stones, glittering teardrops nestled in the middle. Juana looks in the mirror and imagines her younger self—face leaner, skin still creamy, without wrinkles. She smiles as she holds an earring up to her right ear and turns her head slightly to the left to admire it. She knows such things are not what really matters. She wouldn't trade her life with all of its struggles for the expensive emptiness she feels every time she walks into this house. But she is not above enjoying, for a moment, the fantasy of adorning herself with lovely things such as these. Perhaps one day. Then she returns the earrings to the same spot at the back of the drawer and goes back to work.

The guest bedroom rarely gets much use, but Juana dutifully vacuums, dusts, and cleans the bathroom. So far, the woman has stayed downstairs. Perhaps, Juana thinks, she will get lucky and they will switch places for the rest of the day.

She totes the mop and bucket down the stairs and goes back up for the vacuum. On her return trip, halfway down, she slides awkwardly and has to grab for a banister to regain her balance. The weight of the vacuum shifts and she feels a sharp spasm of pain in her shoulder. She pauses for a minute and lets her adrenaline subside. She lifts her arm, testing the shoulder. It throbs but it doesn't seem serious. At least for the moment.

When she reaches the bottom of the stairs she hears whispered giggles coming from the theater.

"No, not tonight. I have to get ready. I'm meeting him in an hour.... At the Skirball. No!...Dave!...Oh, you're so bad...No, I can't...I know. Me too. I'll see you Friday."

Juana has heard versions of this before. It's not her business. But she wonders how people like this *puta* end up in houses like this, while people like her end up cleaning them. She understands she too is a sinner, and it's God's way—*los mansos heredarán la tierra.* But it just doesn't seem right and sometimes it's hard not to question.

Knowing better than to linger, Juana heads into the kitchen, transfers a load of laundry, and sprays the cleaner inside the oven. This needs to sit for a while to do its work. While she waits, she does the counters, puts the dirty dishes in the dishwasher, and scrubs the sinks (both of them). Then she wipes down the refrigerator with the stainless steel cleaner.

To properly reach the back of the oven she has to get down on her knees. It's awkward and again she feels a throb in her shoulder. And that is when she hears the clacking of the footsteps on the marble floor. She looks up and can see the woman standing there, trying to cross behind her to get to the refrigerator.

The woman sighs, exasperated. "Oh, aren't you finished in here yet?"

"Almost, Mrs. Summers."

With a huff, the woman circles back around the other side of the island counter. "Make sure you get all the way inside," she says over her shoulder as she removes a large bottle of vodka from the freezer.

Juana can feel her face flush. The floor is cold and hard against her kneecaps. She closes her eyes and breathes.

"Sí, Mrs. Summers," she says as neutrally as she can.

As she scours the oven, Juana can hear the pinging of ice into the shaker and then the rhythmic shushing. The martinis are starting a little early today. There is a clack on the counter and a trickle as the drink is poured into the glass. She watches surreptitiously as the woman leaves the kitchen. The figure is taut and wiry, muscle fibers clinging doggedly to shoulders and hips. They should be—the woman is always in that gym. But Juana can see that the skin, an artificial reddish bronze, is beginning to hang loosely from the elbows. The woman turns at the stairs and ascends. *Gracias a Dios.*

Juana pushes herself to her feet. The steel shaker sneers at her from the counter where the woman has left it. Her jaw tightens as she rinses it and puts it in the dishwasher. Everything is a test, she tells herself.

Only an hour or so to go. She mops the kitchen and powder room, returns the mop and bucket to the closet, and wheels the vacuum into the remaining area of the first floor. Left to clean are the theater, the den, the gym, and Mr. Summers' office. She vacuums, dusts, and straightens. Heaps of papers cover Mr. Summers' desk, but this, she has been told, is off limits, so, as always, she leaves it undisturbed.

The day is almost over. The final task is to fold the remaining laundry and bring it upstairs. There is no avoiding it. When she enters the bedroom, the woman is standing at the sprawling vanity. Juana can see a wooden box and a lot of expensive jewelry strewn over the countertop. The woman seems agitated, muttering to herself.

"Come on. Where are they?"

Juana waits for a beat and then places the folded clothes on the bed.

"All finished, Mrs. Summers."

"Fine. Fine. Thank you," the woman barks over her shoulder. Then she turns around and shoots Juana a look. She seems to be weighing something in her mind. "Juana, I'm missing a pair of diamond earrings. Did you happen to see them?"

"No, Mrs. Summers."

The woman squints, insinuating.

"Are you sure?"

Juana feels something give inside her. She is tired. She is tired of a lot of things. Who does this *puta* think she is? Maybe she can lie and cheat her way through her own life, and God will be her judge, but what right does she have to accuse others? Juana has earned every single thing she has in this life. She would no sooner steal something than she would jump off a building. She returns the woman's glare with defiance and the moment lingers. In so many ways it's the longest and most intimate conversation the two have ever had.

"No. I didn't see them," Juana says, finally, almost sneering herself.

Then, without waiting for a response, she turns and heads downstairs. She can feel each heartbeat pulse in her ears and her skin is burning. She needs to leave this place quickly before the poison can find its way into her soul. She will find another job, or work two if she has to.

"Hey," she can hear the woman shout behind her.

She goes straight to the little dressing room behind the kitchen, tosses her apron on the floor, and gathers her things. As she returns through the kitchen she can hear the frantic clacking of heels echoing from above. And the woman is yelling.

"You took them, didn't you? You little bitch!" Juana is at the front door when the woman reaches the top of the stairs. "Hey! You get back here! I'm calling the police."

Juana stops and turns. Their eyes lock.

"I want to look in your pockets," the woman hisses.

Juana steels herself, ready for what may come. But as the woman starts to rush down the stairs one of her heels slips. Time freezes as Juana watches the legs fly out and forward in slow motion. After the rear end hits, the back of the head slams into the marble with tremendous force. The head hits again on a lower step before the body comes to rest in an awkward, twisted shape, the hair splayed out in a kind of mane. In a moment Juana can see blood start to seep out from underneath it. She stands there for a minute, watching, transfixed. Then, without thinking about it, she finds herself sitting down with her back against the foyer wall, elbows wrapped around her knees, the wall cool against her back. The blood is coming thicker now, in an ever-increasing semi-circle. The woman's leg twitches rhythmically.

Juana knows she should do something to help, but she doesn't move. Random memories begin to enter her mind. Her mother, sobbing uncontrollably when the soldiers came and took Pablito away. The sourness of the coyote's breath as he grunted on top of her. The squeals of Mari and Jesus when she surprised them and brought home the puppy. She thinks about God and all the times she has wavered in her faith. All the ways the world has challenged it. And she has held on.

Gradually, the woman's leg stops twitching. Juana begins to focus and an idea starts to form in her head. *Sí. El Señor da y el Señor quita.*

She can do it and be gone in a minute. No one will see her, unless Mr. Summers comes home early, which he never does. And the woman said she was meeting him somewhere tonight, did she not? Juana knows they will question her about the accident. Maybe even try to blame her somehow. But she has been watching *Dateline* for years. It's one of her guilty pleasures. It helped her practice her English. What will they be able to prove? That her fingerprints are all over the house? Of course, they are—she works there. Time of death? That is a window. She will tell them that when she left the house the woman was just fine, upstairs getting dressed. She has no idea what caused the accident. *Sí, Señor policeman. I leaving 3:30. No, I no see anything. Sí, Mrs. Summers, she drink the vodka a lot.* They will check the security cameras and see that she told them the truth. They will have no reason not to believe her.

But first, she must make sure the woman is really dead. Juana stands and moves close to the body, taking care to step around the expanding pool of blood. It is a rich, red velvet carpet on the cold stone. The chest is still. She waits and watches for a little while more, but there is no doubt.

This time, when Juana walks up the stairs the steps feel lighter, the pain in her hip somehow less. She reaches the top and heads directly for the woman's bedroom and the vanity drawer.

She will not try to sell them. And if anyone ever notices them missing, there will be no way to connect them to her. Perhaps she will wear them one single time, when she is much older, and all is forgotten, and she and Mauricio go out for a special dinner. Until then they will stay in her pouch, in her shoebox, under some old letters, at the top of her closet.

Before she leaves the house, Juana turns and looks it over one more time. Yes, very clean.

Teenage Dirtbag
Wheatus

Teenage Dirtbag is a song by American rock band Wheatus, released on June 20, 2000, as the lead single from their eponymous debut album. The song was written by guitarist and vocalist Brendan B. Brown and was inspired by a childhood experience of his.

Despite being a huge success in the UK, Europe and Australia, it failed to chart on the US *Billboard Hot 100*, peaking only at #7 in the Alternative Songs chart.

The 2nd verse of the song was originally subjected to censorship, which eventually resulted in the band re-recording and re-releasing the song in 2020, retaining the original lyrics.

Teenage Dirtbag

Barb Goffman

Long Island, New York. May 1985.

"Dude, that girl's so outta your league, she's batting four hundred for the majors, while you're warming the Little League bench."

I gave Justin major side-eye. "Yeah, like we ever play sports."

"My point exactly," he said.

It was a sunny May morning. Justin and I were walking the track at our high school. Our gym teacher had mentally checked out a few weeks before, only doing the minimum required, waiting for that glorious day in June when school would let out for summer. He still worked with the jocks, of course. But he ignored kids like Justin and me, kids whose idea of athletics was calculating the odds of who'd win a game, as long as we circled the track. "Getting some exercise," he called it.

I kept staring at Noelle. For the past half hour, she and some other girls had been doing lunges, squats, and kicks on the field inside the track. Boy, was she flexible. *Focus on her face, Brian. You don't need to get a hard-on now.* Okay, her face. Her beautiful heart-shaped face. Between her plump lips, her adorable dimples, and her blue eyes—dark like ripe blueberries—she was it for me.

"Did you hand in your class choices for next year?" Justin asked. "How many APs did you decide to take?"

I heard him ask about advanced placement classes, but it barely registered. "What kills me," I said, "isn't that Noelle'll never notice me. It's that she's dating that asswipe Travis. She deserves so much better."

Justin sighed loudly. "Dude, you need to let this go. She's a cheerleader. He's a scouted shortstop. You don't exist in their world."

Like he had to tell me that. Justin and I were short, skinny nerds who played Dungeons & Dragons with our friends on the weekends. The only reason Travis knew me is because we lived on the same block. During elementary school, I was invited to all his birthday parties—no doubt at his parents' insistence. By the time junior high rolled around, he regularly stole my lunch money, not because he needed it but because he could. Because he was a jerk, to me and lots of other kids. At least I didn't have to see him on the bus anymore. He'd gotten a cherry-red IROC-Z for his seventeenth birthday a couple of months ago, and he drove it to school every day, peeling around corners like he ruled the world.

But Noelle…she wasn't stuck-up at all. We were in the same health class last fall, and she'd always seemed sweet as pie and had the cutest chirpy voice. What she saw in Travis, I'd never know.

Mr. Gordon blew his whistle. Time to head inside.

"Did you say something about APs?" I asked.

Justin rolled his eyes. "Yeah. How many next year?"

"Three: calc, chem, and bio." I'd thought about taking Advanced Placement English next year too, but my parents said I shouldn't overload my schedule. Better to have time to enjoy my senior year. "You?"

"The same, plus French."

"Noelle takes French, doesn't she?" *What would it be like to French-kiss Noelle?*

"Damn, you've got it bad, dude."

We were walking about twenty yards behind Noelle and her friends. She was wearing tight gray pants—I think my sister called them *leggings*—with a neon-pink crop top and white Keds. Then she pulled off her headband and shook out her chocolate-brown hair. It fell in curly waves around her petite shoulders. *I wonder if it's as silky as it looks.*

I had to take a physics test next period. I knew the material inside and out, but that wouldn't matter now. I'd never be able to concentrate.

Yeah, dude. I had it bad.

✶✶✶✶✶

Two periods later I headed outside for lunch, carrying a tray with a slice of Sicilian pizza, an apple, and a can of Sprite. When we had good weather, our school let us eat in a large open-air courtyard with long picnic tables.

As usual, Travis and his obnoxious friends were sitting on—not at, but on—two tables pushed together near the door, looking down on the rest of us as if they were royalty and we were peons. Every day I had to walk right past them to reach the table where I always ate with Justin and the rest of my friends. And every day I heard Travis and his crew make vile comments that made me long for graduation next year, for never having to see their ugly mugs again. The only thing that made it better was when Noelle sat with them. She didn't come to lunch every day. But when she did, like today, the world had a softness to it. I'd focus on her glowing face as I passed their tables and could ignore everything else. Most of the time. But sometimes Travis was too obnoxious to ignore.

"Check out that rack." Travis leered at some girl with red hair who was heading this way. How did everyone not see what a prick he was?

"Tasty," his friend Paul said. He and Travis wore their brown hair short in the front and long in the back, in that current style I could never pull off without looking like a dork.

"Damn straight," Travis said. The girl was coming close, but they weren't lowering their voices at all. "She must be new, because, man, I sure would've remembered those."

Not *her*. But *those*. Classy.

Noelle stomped in front of him and smacked his chest with the back of her hand. "I'm right here."

Travis sneered. "Chill out. You're such a drama queen."

"And you're such a dick," she said.

"What did you call me?" Travis grabbed her arm, and she winced.

Maybe if I'd been thinking clearly—if Noelle hadn't been on my

159

brain all morning—I would've stayed out of it. But I dropped my tray on the closest table and charged over there, getting up in Travis's face. "Let go of her."

He did, leaping off the table and grabbing my black shirt instead. Now, instead of eye to eye, we were eye to neck. He was a foot taller than me. "What the fuck do you want, loser?"

My mind went blank. Travis outweighed me by at least fifty pounds and could pound me into oblivion. *Say something, idiot.* But I had nothing.

Travis shoved me away. "Look at this dirtbag in his Iron Maiden T-shirt, trying to tell me what to do."

"Like anyone listens to Iron Maiden," Paul said, stepping down from the table. "The Boss rules!"

"Yeah, he rules!" Travis high-fived him.

I swallowed hard. They didn't know what they were talking about. Iron Maiden was way cooler than Springsteen. Iron Maiden was my only nod to coolness.

"Still got nothing to say, dipshit?" Travis laughed, then turned to Noelle. "Figures your knight in shining armor would be nothing but a big chicken. *Buk buk buk!*"

He flapped his arms as lots of kids laughed and Noelle stared at the ground. She couldn't even look at me. I felt my cheeks flush. Tears coming. I had to get out of there. I turned tail and ran into the building, hating myself, hating that I was proving Travis's point. I was nothing but a big fat chicken.

*****

I was still hiding out in a nearby restroom twenty minutes later. *Why had I made a bad situation worse by running?* That's when Travis and Paul came inside. I could see them through the gap between the stall and its door.

"Hey, I didn't tell you," Travis said while they were taking care of business. "My uncle Gary came over last night."

"The one in the army?" Paul asked.

"Yeah. He's on leave. He apologized for not being here for my big birthday and gave me a Ruger Mark Two as a belated gift."

"No shit," Paul said.

A gun? Who gets a gun for a birthday present?

"Man, you've gotta see it," Travis said. "Silver top, brown pistol grip, ten-round magazine. My dad's gonna take me to the range this weekend for target practice."

"I'll come over after school." Paul zipped up.

"No time today. After I drop my stuff off I've gotta grab my game bag, then book it to the shop for a couple of hours. Busy season. Then tonight we're playing Huntington."

"Right, I forgot," Paul said.

Travis's parents owned a sports- and camping-equipment franchise, and they ran the flagship store here in town. Last year I went in there with my mom, looking for golf clubs for my dad's birthday. Travis was leaning against a counter, his face all smarmy, as he chatted up some girls who acted like playing on the school baseball team was the most important thing in the world.

Travis joined Paul at the sinks. "Tomorrow night should work."

"You should sneak the gun into school tomorrow," Paul said. "Show it off."

"No way, man. Principal Vargas is a real hard-ass about the no-tolerance policy. I can't risk getting expelled and losing my chance at a scholarship."

Paul nodded. "Okay, then call me when you get home from the game tonight. I'll come by."

"Damn, you have a boner for this gun." Travis laughed. "I get it. You have a lame pellet gun, and I've got the real deal. But you're just gonna have to wait till tomorrow night, man. No doubt I'm gonna get sucked into a long phone call with Noelle tonight about what just happened out there. How I *treated her*." He rolled his eyes.

"Girls," Paul said in a more subdued tone. "Ain't hardly worth the trouble."

"You know it. But I'll just pour on the charm and tell her I was worried about today's game. She'll feel so sorry for me, she'll forgive anything, as usual. Then she'll come over and put out." He shrugged. "If need be, I'll buy her another piece of cheap jewelry this weekend."

Paul chuckled. "I'll have to remember those moves."

"If Noelle weren't so bodacious"—Travis held out his hands as if he were cupping two grapefruits—"I would've cut her loose months ago."

That freaking pig. I kicked my sneaker against the tile floor and then could've kicked myself. *Did they hear me?* I held my breath.

"How *did* you score a chick who likes to climb in your bedroom window?" Paul asked.

"I'm a God, my man, that's all there is to it. Maybe if you start leaving your bedroom window unlocked all the time, you'll get lucky too."

"You think?"

"Yeah, though knowing you, Fat Felicia would climb in." Travis shivered. "Come on, let's go."

As the door swung closed behind them, I stood there with my lip curled and my palms burning. In my anger, I'd dug my nails into the skin, drawing blood. Travis was the one who deserved pain. Not me. Not Noelle. If she learned how he'd been manipulating her, she'd cut *him* loose. *I should tell her.*

But I couldn't. Considering how I let Travis rag on me and then ran like a baby, she must think I'm a coward. I needed to forget about her.

But don't forget about him, dude. I could practically hear Justin's voice in my head. Travis deserved to pay for hurting Noelle. For using her. For playing mind games with her. And for the pain he'd caused so many dweebs like me.

A smile grew on my face. I knew exactly how to do it.

*****

Every time I walked the few blocks to Justin's, I passed Travis's house. As I neared it now, I looked for his car. It wasn't parked in his usual spot in the driveway. He'd obviously come and gone in the time it took me to take the bus home, drop off my books, and head back out. The house should be empty.

I casually glanced around, checking for kids riding their bikes or moms pushing strollers. Satisfied I was alone, I ducked under the shade of a dogwood tree in Travis's front yard, its pink-and-white blossoms reminding me of Noelle, small yet vibrant and beautiful. Then I hurried toward the side of the house.

In first grade, Travis showed off his bedroom during his birthday party. While a dozen boys had crowded around him, mesmerized by his new Evel Knievel stunt game, I'd been pushed up against a window. It was annoying then but helpful now. I could pick out his window. The ladder Noelle used to sneak inside had to be nearby.

And there it was. Not an actual ladder but close enough: a white trellis with ivy climbing up one edge. I probably didn't weigh much more than Noelle. If it could hold her, it would hold me. I hoped.

I started climbing. On the fifth rung the trellis creaked, and I stopped dead. *Please don't crack.* But it held firm. I kept going. I prayed Travis hadn't exaggerated, that he really did leave his bedroom window unlocked all the time. If not, my plan would be toast.

When I reached the top, I glanced around. No prying eyes from the next-door neighbor. It was now or never. The window slid up quickly and quietly, just as Travis had said. In moments, I was in.

The place stank like a locker room. Dirty baseball uniforms lay in a heap on the silvery-blue carpeting, along with lots of other clothes and Travis's backpack. Sports memorabilia cluttered his desk, and trophies were crowded on his dresser. But where was the gun?

Funny, I'd thought his new toy would be sitting front and center. I checked out the closet. Nothing interesting in there. Opened the bedside table drawer. Certs breath mints, condoms, and a stiff sock. *Ewww.* I moved on to the dresser. Inside the top drawer were underwear and jock straps. *I'm not looking under those.* I slammed the drawer shut and heard a noise. Jingling. What was that?

Oh God. Was someone home?

I dashed across the large room toward the window as someone

padded down the hall, hurrying this way—and the door to Travis's room was wide open. I wasn't fast enough. No time to clamber onto the windowsill. I needed a story to explain my presence, but what?

The footsteps and jingling stopped. My mind went blank. Boy, I sucked under pressure. Praying for a miracle, I turned around.

It was a dog. A golden retriever. He was smiling at me.

Thank God. My adrenaline waning, I slid down onto the carpet, exhausted. The dog trotted over, his tags jingling some more. A bone-shaped one revealed his name. "Hi, Bo." I petted him, and he licked my nose. "Do you know where Travis put his gun?"

It seemed like he wanted to tell me but couldn't get the words out. I continued to pet him while I looked around the room. The walls were covered with posters of sports stars, sports cars, and wet women in bikinis—which made me think of my cousin Kenny. He had bikini-shot posters just like these, and he hid dirty magazines under his bed.

I reached under Travis's bed. *Penthouse. Playboy.* Was I the only kid in America who didn't hide dirty magazines in his room? My dreams of Noelle were more than enough to get me through the night. I reached under the bed again and grabbed something small and rectangular. A box of bullets. This was encouraging. And…bingo! I pulled out a yellow cardboard box that said Ruger on the top and Mark II Pistol on the side.

I opened the box of bullets. Ten were missing, which meant Travis must have loaded the pistol. Thank God for small favors. I'd never held a gun before. I didn't know how to load it and hadn't been looking forward to figuring it out.

After lifting the gun from its box, I shoved the box and everything else back under the bed and carefully carried the pistol over to Travis's backpack. It was as cluttered as his room, filled with textbooks, notebooks, candy wrappers, a baseball, and a T-shirt. I buried the gun deep in the bottom of the bag, under the shirt. Knowing Travis, he wouldn't do any homework tonight. He'd never even know the gun was in there when he went to school tomorrow.

And now, I just had to wait.

*****

The next day, with eight minutes left in physics, I got a bathroom pass and hurried to the pay phone by the gym. It was right off the hall where all the science classes were held, which made things easy.

I pulled a slip of paper from my pocket. I'd written the school's number on it last night. Now I dropped a quarter into the phone. No one was around, but I still planned to whisper. When the office secretary answered, I said in as deep a voice as I could muster, "Travis Skalbeck has a loaded gun in his backpack. He—"

"We've heard, and it's being taken care of. Who am I speaking with?"

I hung up the phone. They'd heard? Someone must have seen it. Now he'd be expelled.

Yes! I pumped a fist above my head. Who was the dirtbag now?!

*****

Ten minutes later I rushed through the cafeteria hot-lunch line. I couldn't wait to see Principal Vargas drag Travis away. But when I got to the courtyard, things were weird. No Travis. No Paul. No Noelle. The remaining cool kids were sitting at their picnic tables—actually sitting at them, not on them. They were whispering to each other. In fact, everyone in the courtyard was talking with their heads together. The air was buzzing with excitement.

"What's going on?" I asked Justin and Lance as I sat at our usual table.

"Two periods ago, in the middle of English, Vargas showed up at my classroom with a cop." Lance's bushy eyebrows rose on that last word. "The cop marched up to Travis Jerkwad Skalbeck, snatched his book bag off the floor, and took him into the hall."

"Word is he had a loaded gun in there," Justin said.

"And he's been arrested." Lance sported a huge grin.

Back in junior high, Travis pushed Lance into his locker one day and slammed the door shut. Lance wasn't in there long. A teacher heard him banging on it. But Lance had hated Travis ever since. From the delight on most faces throughout the courtyard, he wasn't the only one. It reminded me of summer days as a kid when an ice cream truck would drive by the house and Mom would hand me a couple of dollars. Pure unexpected joy.

"Dude, after what Travis did to you yesterday, you must be thrilled," Justin said to me.

"More like ecstatic," Lance said. "Right?"

"Hell yeah," I said. They'd seen what happened here, and I'd talked to Justin about it last night—omitting what I'd overheard in the bathroom, as well as my trip to Travis's after school. Best to keep those secrets to myself. I was sorry I didn't get to see him dragged off by the cops, but I could picture it, and that was better than any dirty magazine.

Our friend Dave set his tray on the table. "Wait till you hear my news."

"We heard," Lance said. "Travis the Terrible is finally getting what he deserves."

"I don't know what he was thinking, bringing a loaded gun to school," Justin said.

"He probably acted surprised, like he didn't do it on purpose," I said. "Any lie to cover his ass." I was getting better at lying too.

"There's so much more going on." Dave leaned forward, his acned face eager with anticipation. "I have a test tomorrow in Hebrew, but Mr. Bernstein knew I didn't need the refresher he was giving today, so he sent me down to the office to do some photocopying for him. Noelle Shuldberg came in to speak to Principal Vargas while I was in there. He left his office door open, so I heard everything. She told Vargas that Travis threatened to shoot Paul Feder."

"Holy shit," Justin said.

Holy shit indeed.

"Wait," Lance said, "why would he threaten to kill his best friend?"

Dave laughed. "Yesterday after school, Paul hit on Noelle. Fed her some sob story about how lonely he was. Basically begged her to have sex with him. Said it could be their 'little secret.'"

"No way," I said.

"Yes way," Dave said. "Noelle got all offended. Said she wasn't that kind of girl."

Lance barked out a laugh.

"Hey," I said. "You don't know she's lying."

They all gave me a *come-on* look, and I exhaled loudly. "There's a big difference between fooling around with your boyfriend and screwing around with his best friend." To this, they all nodded.

"Anyway," Dave said, "she told Travis what Paul did. Travis got so mad, he said he'd kill Paul. Noelle thought he was kidding, but then during homeroom, she poked through Travis's backpack for a pen and saw the gun. She told Principal Vargas she was so worried, she had to rat him out."

"Ohhhh," Justin said. "This explained the fight Travis and Paul had this morning. With everything else going on, I nearly forgot. When I got off the bus, they were shoving each other in the parking lot. Fists flying. Two teachers broke it up, but Travis kept yelling, 'I know what you did! You're dead to me!' And Paul said something weird about preferring to have a 'fat girlfriend and a lame pellet gun than a best friend who treated him like crap.'"

Whoa. I knew exactly what that meant. As I debated sharing what I'd overheard in the restroom yesterday, Lance's eyes went wide. Someone tapped me on the shoulder. I twisted around to find Noelle standing there.

"Hi, Brian," she said. "Can I talk to you? Alone?"

I'm dreaming. That explains all of this.

"Brian…?"

Justin elbowed me in the ribs and whispered, "Dude."

Guess I'm not dreaming.

"Sure, Noelle." I just said her name out loud *to her*. I followed her to an empty picnic table at a deserted end of the courtyard, all the while thinking, *I'm about to talk to Noelle, and she's going to talk to me. This is really happening.*

She gave me a shy smile as we sat down. "I wanted to thank you for what you did for me yesterday. That was brave, standing up to Travis like that."

I swallowed hard, once again not sure what to say. I needed to work on that. I settled on "sure" with a lame shrug.

"You probably heard what happened this morning," she said. "Travis getting arrested."

I nodded. *Get a grip, Brian. This is your chance to talk to her. Find some freaking words.*

"It never would have happened without you," she said.

"Come again?"

"I figured, if you could stand up to Travis, I could too. But I'm not good at talking in stressful situations. It's why I kept my mouth shut yesterday when he said all those mean things to you. I'm sorry about that. I was so ashamed of myself."

That's why? I'd misread the whole situation. "You're doing fine."

Noelle squeezed my hand, and I could have died happily right then.

"Thanks," she said. "I'm better with writing. That's what I'm supposed to be doing now. I joined the literary magazine a few months ago, and some of us meet twice a week at lunch in Mr. Flora's classroom. We write and talk about poetry and short stories."

"Wow. That's cool." I'd had no idea she was creative.

She smiled again. "After you were so brave yesterday, I decided to end things with Travis. I'd been thinking about it for a while. No more Travis. No more hanging with his crew. I have a lot more in common with my lit-mag friends. So I wrote Travis a letter and went over to leave it on his bed. That's...when I saw you climbing out his window."

I broke out in a cold sweat.

"I should have said something," Noelle continued, "but I was still embarrassed, so I hid behind a dogwood tree. You walked right past me. Anyway, when I went into his room, I realized I had more to say in my letter about the mind games he liked to play with me, so I rummaged in his backpack for a pen, and I saw the gun. You put it in there, didn't you?" Her eyes bugged out as my mouth dropped open.

"You're pale as death. Don't worry. I didn't tell anyone, and I'm not going to. This is our secret."

Our secret? Noelle and I were seriously going to have a secret?

"You don't say a lot, do you?" she asked. "I hardly ever do either, but you bring the chatterbox out of me."

"That happens when people click." *Did I just say that to her?*

She nodded. "How did you know about the gun?"

I guessed it was honesty day, for both of us. "I was in a bathroom stall yesterday when Travis and Paul came in. They talked about the gun and some other stuff." No reason to tell her the nasty things they'd said about her. She was rid of him already and on her own terms too. That was enough.

"So you decided to get revenge by hiding the gun in his backpack and then..." She tilted her head questioningly.

"I called in an anonymous tip that he brought it to school."

"That's kind of what I figured."

"But when I did it, they already knew."

"Yeah, that was because of me. I told the principal I saw the gun in his backpack."

"I heard. I actually heard about your whole conversation with Principal Vargas."

"You did? Wow, word travels fast."

"We're lucky Travis didn't look for the gun last night to go after Paul."

"That's not luck. I knew when Travis got home from the game last night, he'd want to pull the gun out. The night before, he'd actually caressed it while I was over there."

Talk about having a boner for that pistol.

"If he'd realized the gun wasn't in the box," she said, "he would've searched for it, and that could've been the end of your plan. I wanted the plan to work. No, I *needed* it to work. I'm tired of the way he treats people. So I didn't leave my letter yesterday afternoon. Instead, around nine last night, when I knew he'd be getting home from the game, I slipped out of my house and went back over there. My parents are on vacation, and my grandma's staying with me. She goes to sleep really early. Never checks on me. She trusts me. I guess I don't deserve it." She raised, then dropped one shoulder. "Anyway, I went over there last night and…distracted him."

Did she mean…? From the way she was blushing, it seemed she did.

"His bedroom door locks, and if his parents don't know I'm there and he says he's going to sleep early…" Now she shrugged both shoulders. "We put the TV on like usual, and they didn't hear anything. I didn't want to, especially since I'd finally decided to end things, but it was all I could think of."

I stared at the table. "You're really pretty"—now my cheeks warmed too—"so it's no surprise you could distract him from the gun and from going after Paul, who was a total slimeball to you." I glanced back up in time to see her shake her head.

"Oh, no. I didn't tell Travis last night about what Paul did. The timing had to be just right. I stayed till Travis fell asleep. Then this morning I called him before school and told him how Paul treated me like a slut yesterday. I figured Travis would get into it with Paul today, but he wouldn't bring the gun to school. He's too afraid of losing the baseball scholarships he's sure will come. But Principal Vargas doesn't know that."

"Dang. You called me brave before, but you were pretty brave to do all that. And crafty, getting revenge on him and Paul at the same time."

"Thanks. Considering the rest of his life is about to fall apart, Travis isn't going to be happy when I break up with him. That's next." She stared at the bruise he left on her arm yesterday. I bet it wasn't the first one. "But hopefully he won't be able to hurt me—or anybody else—anymore." She chuckled. "He must still be wondering how the gun ended up in his backpack."

We stared at each other. She looked as awkward as I felt. "I should let you get to your lit-mag friends."

"Are you going to junior prom in two weeks?" Noelle said it quickly.

Nervously.

My lower lip shook. *Is she asking me to prom?* "I hadn't planned on it."

She started unbuttoning her shirt. I thought I would pass out until I realized she was wearing a white tank top underneath it. An Iron Maiden shirt.

"They're playing at Nassau Coliseum the same night as prom," she said, "and I've got two tickets. I was going to drag my friend Jenny along, but Iron Maiden's not her thing. She's a Tears for Fears kind of girl. I'm hoping you might want to go instead?"

"I'd love to." I broke into a huge grin. "I'll try to think of more things to say by then."

She laughed. "Good. I'm looking forward to it. After all, we dirtbags have to stick together."

Flippin' the 45s

Vinnie Hansen fled the winds of the South Dakota prairie and headed for the California coast the day after high school graduation. A two-time Claymore Award finalist, she is the author of the Carol Sabala mystery series, the novels *Lostart Street* and *One Gun*, as well as over fifty published short works. Still sane(ish) after 27 years of teaching high school English, Vinnie has retired and plays keyboards with ukulele groups in Santa Cruz, California, where she lives with her husband and the requisite cat. For news and updates, visit https://www.vinniehansen.com/

Jeanne DuBois taught for many years at the district elementary school for Deaf and Hard of Hearing students in Gainesville, Florida. She mainstreamed many of those students into her fifth-grade classes. Some brought interpreters. Others wore various kinds of hearing aids. Once, she forgot to turn off her RF transmitter. The student with the receiver heard her dissing the school lunch. He teased her forever after. "Was your lunch all yellow again today, Mrs. DuBois?!" Her stories have been published in several anthologies, including *Moonlight & Misadventure*, and *Peace, Love & Crime: Crime Fiction Inspired by the Music of the '60s*. For news and updates visit: jeanne-dubois.com

Josh Pachter has been writing, editing, and translating short crime fiction since his 1968 debut appearance in *Ellery Queen's Mystery Magazine*. In 2023, fifty-five years later, Genius Book Publishing released his first novel, *Dutch Threat*, and *First Week Free at the Roomy Toilet*, a chapter-book mystery for younger readers, will be published by Level Best in 2024. The most recent of the twenty anthologies he's edited was *Happiness Is a Warm Gun: Crime Fiction Inspired by the Songs of the Beatles* (Down and Out,

2023). In 2020, the Short Mystery Fiction Society awarded him its Golden Derringer for Lifetime Achievement. The idea of a book of stories inspired by one-hit wonders was originally his. He proposed it as a joke, but Jay Hartman took the suggestion seriously, and *now* look what's happened! *www.joshpachter.com*

J. M. Taylor spins his sinister fantasies in Boston where he lives with his wife and son. He has appeared in *Tough, Wildside Black Cat,* and *AHMM,* among others. His books include *Night of the Furies,* from New Pulp Press, *Dark Heat,* from Genretarium, and *No Score* from Unnerving. When he's not writing, he teaches under an assumed name. You can find him at jmtaylorcrimewriter.com and on Facebook at *Night of the Furies.*

Christine Verstraete is a Wisconsin writer who enjoys writing about monsters to mysteries. Her stories have been published in various anthologies and magazines including, *Scare Street: Night Terrors. Vol. 26, The Colored Lens, Run from the Dead, A to Z of Horror: O is for Outbreak,* and others. She is the author of the *Lizzie Borden, Zombie Hunter* series. Learn more at her blog: https://girlzombieauthors.blogspot.com and website: www.cverstraete.com.

Sandra Murphy lives in St Louis with Ozzie the Westie impersonator dog and Louie the tuxedo cat who pretends he's James Bond. Both have learned to keep a low profile when Sandra is talking to her imaginary friends. Ozzie and Louie make her stories better with their astute comments and eye rolls. Sandra also writes magazine articles, edits a newsletter, and may someday write a book. If not a respectable job, at least it keeps her off the streets and out of the bars.

Joseph S. Walker lives in Indiana and teaches college literature and composition courses. His short fiction has appeared in *Alfred Hitchcock's Mystery Magazine, Ellery Queen's Mystery Magazine,*

Mystery Weekly, Tough, and a number of other magazines and anthologies, including *Best American Mystery and Suspense* and three consecutive editions of *The Mysterious Bookshop Presents the Best Mystery Stories of the Year.* He has been nominated for the Edgar Award and the Derringer Award and has won the Bill Crider Prize for Short Fiction. He also won the Al Blanchard Award in 2019 and 2021. Visit his website at https://jswalkerauthor.com/

Wendy Harrison is a retired prosecutor who turned to short mystery fiction during the pandemic. Her stories have been published in numerous anthologies including *Peace, Love & Crime, Autumn Noir, Crimeucopia, The Big Fang, Gargoylicon,* and *Death of a Bad Neighbour* as well as in *Shotgun Honey.* When Hurricane Ian destroyed her home in Florida, she moved to Washington State, as far from Florida as she could get.

Bev Vincent is the author of several non-fiction books, including *The Road to the Dark Tower* and *Stephen King: A Complete Exploration of His Work, Life, and Influences.* He co-edited the anthology *Flight or Fright* with King and has published over 130 stories, with appearances in *Ellery Queen's, Alfred Hitchcock's* and *Black Cat Mystery Magazines.* His work has been published in over twenty languages and nominated for the Stoker (twice), Edgar, Locus, Ignotus, Rondo Hatton Classic Horror and ITW Thriller Awards. To learn more, visit bevvincent.com

Leone Ciporin's short stories have appeared in *The Saturday Evening Post, Black Cat Mystery Magazine, Mystery Weekly, Woman's World,* and several mystery anthologies. She currently serves as secretary for the Mid-Atlantic chapter of Mystery Writers of America. Leone lives in Charlottesville, Va.

Adam Gorgoni was born and raised in New York City and is a graduate of Harvard University where he studied Latin American History and US Foreign Policy. He makes his home in Los Angeles where, when he is not on the tennis court, he is a professional music composer and producer. His film scoring credits include Sundance favorite *Starting Out In The Evening*, Deauville Grand Prize winner *The Dead Girl*, and cult comedy classic *Waiting*. Television work: USA Network's *Necessary Roughness*, the CW series *Aliens In America*, Lorne Michaels' ABC comedy *Sons and Daughters*, as well as shows for NBC, HBO, Discovery Channel, Bravo, and National Geographic. Adam has extensive experience in music for advertising, with clients such as Toyota, AT&T, IBM, and Mastercard. He served as a co-producer of the ground breaking musical Head Over Heels, which debuted on Broadway in 2018.

In recent years (i.e. the pandemic) he has returned to an old love, crime fiction, and is currently revising his first novel. "Bitch" is his first published story and he is thrilled to have it appear in *One Hit Wonders*, not least because his wife co-wrote the 1997 Meredith Brooks song from which the story takes its name.

Barb Goffman wrote *Teenage Dirtbag* as a tribute to her fellow Gen Xers and John Hughes movies. She's been nominated for major US crime fiction awards forty times (including seventeen Agatha nominations—a category record) and has won the Agatha Award three times, the Macavity Award twice, and the Anthony Award, Silver Falchion Award, and Ellery Queen Readers Award once each. She's also been a finalist for the Derringer Award and the Thriller Award, and she's had stories on the Other Distinguished Mystery and Suspense list in the two most-recent volumes of *The Best American Mystery and Suspense*. Her stories have appeared in *Alfred Hitchcock's Mystery Magazine*, *Black Cat Mystery Magazine*, *Black Cat Weekly*, *Ellery Queen's Mystery Magazine*, *Sherlock Holmes Mystery Magazine*, and many anthologies. When not writing, Barb makes her living as a freelance crime-fiction editor. She especially enjoys working on traditional and cozy mysteries. Learn more at www.barbgoffman.com.

Made in United States
Orlando, FL
15 January 2024

42458748R00104